A SHOT!

A shot had struck the safe door. . . .

Instinctively he rolled to the side just as another shot ripped above him and plunked into a blackened wall stud that poked out above the foundation. John was covered immediately with black, gummy ash. Diving behind a heap of rubble, he drew his Colt.

He had seen the powder smoke of that last shot. Someone was firing at him from the forest. Popping up like a gallery target, he fired a quick shot toward the spot from where the fire had come.

His bullet ripped harmlessly through the trees. Immediately two other quick shots rang out from some distance over, and John felt the lead sing past his ear. He dropped down again, teeth gritted. That had been far too close.

"Who are you?" he hollered. "What do you want?"

The only answer was silence.

Other *Leisure* books by Will Cade:
FLEE THE DEVIL
THE GALLOWSMAN

WILL CADE

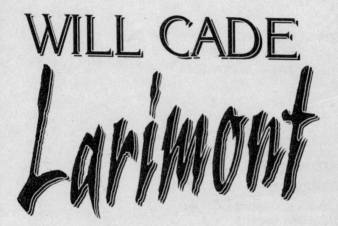

Larimont

LEISURE BOOKS NEW YORK CITY

To Kate.

A LEISURE BOOK®

October 1999

Published by

Dorchester Publishing Co., Inc.
276 Fifth Avenue
New York, NY 10001

ISBN 0-8439-4618-0

The name "Leisure Books" and the stylized "L" with design are trademarks of Dorchester Publishing Co., Inc.

Printed in the United States of America.

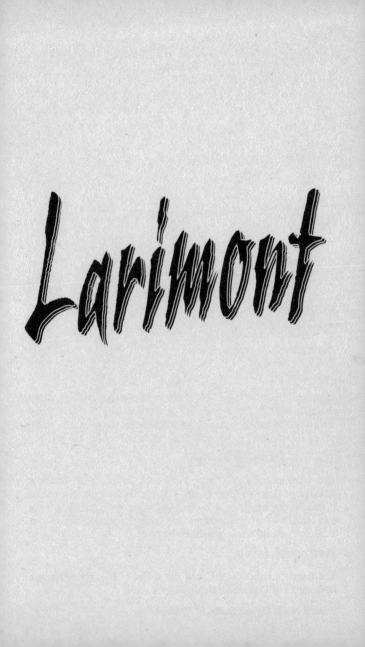

Larimont

Chapter One

John Kenton wiped dust from the passenger
car window and looked out across the Colorado landscape. There it was, the town of
Larimont, looking no different than it had the
last time he had seen it, with its weathered and
grayish buildings standing with backs to the
mountains and fronts facing a wide street of
yellow dust. In the background of it all the
mountains loomed high and circled toward
each other, joining to form a sort of vast open-
ended ring all about the town, enclosing it in a
slate-colored wall of stone and dirt, dotted
with evergreens up its lower half, barren at the
summits.

The same old town of his boyhood . . . but

different now, because one who had always been here no longer was, and never would be again.

The train continued its wide arc toward the town, winding through the natural gateway that provided the only good entrance to the Larimont Valley. John glanced over to the other side of the train car and out the sooty window toward the road that ran roughly parallel to the tracks. A flatbed wagon rolled along, sending up a double cloud of dust behind the wheels. The wagon's driver lazily waved toward the train, greeting passengers he couldn't possibly see from that distance. John Kenton smiled. This was indeed Larimont, the Larimont he had known since childhood, the hometown he could never quite put behind him.

In the midst of all this humdrum, marvelously routine normality, it was very hard for John to really believe his father was dead, and that this homecoming would be the first at which his father would not be standing on the station platform to greet him. With the sun bright and the wind stirring across the mountains, with Larimont's streets full of people going about the same daily routines they had done for fifteen years, how was a man supposed to realize that his father was dead and buried?

The station platform came into view, and John picked out the familiar form of Victoria Rivers standing among the handful of people upon it.

The train sent out a long and piercing wail, followed by a loud screeching as the noisy brakes engaged. John stood, picking up his carpetbag, and stepped down the aisle and out onto the platform. Victoria, a distinguished, dark-haired woman who retained both her beautiful face and impressive figure despite fifty or more years of living, approached him, her arms extended.

Seeing her made John happy, yet all the more sad at the same time. He wasn't used to seeing Victoria Rivers without his father at her side. The two had courted each other for years since John's mother had died, and there had been a lot of serious talk about marriage. Only a piece of paper and a wedding ring had separated Victoria from being John's stepmother.

"Hello, Victoria. It's good to see you."

"And it's good to see you, John." Victoria wrapped her arms around the slender young man and squeezed him hard. "I'm so glad you could get away to spend some time here. And I'm sorry you couldn't get here in time for Bill's funeral." She smiled in a very sad way. "But on second thought, I guess it's just as well. That fool preacher did his best to make the service as sorrowful as possible. And I have to say, he did a pretty good job of it."

"How are you doing, Victoria?" John asked. He'd noted that she talked too fast and too furious, her words rushing out in a torrent—something she normally didn't do. He suspected she was trying not to cry.

For a moment a tear glistened in her eye. "I'm as well as I can be at a time like this. How about you?"

John shrugged. "The same." He looked around him. "But you know, even now it really is good to be home. It makes me feel a little better, somehow."

"I'm glad, John. And now, let's get you checked into the Donaho. A lot of folks got off that train, and they might just rush the place."

John walked with Victoria to her buggy, which was hitched and waiting beside the station house. He tossed his bag in the rear and helped her to the rider's side, then unhitched the horse and climbed up to the driver's seat. He took the reins in hand, clicked his tongue, and the buggy began rolling down the dusty road and deeper into town.

The grayness of the town, which had been so evident from the train, wasn't as obvious up close, particularly since the street ran by the fronts of the buildings, which were kept painted, unlike the rear sections visible from the train.

The grief that had weighed on John like a heavy cloak lifted a bit further as he looked around him. As he had on the train, he realized just how much he had missed his hometown. The picture of it had always been in the back of his mind, coming out into his consciousness only occasionally, usually at the times he was lonely.

Though he loved Larimont, John still had no regrets that he'd left it. He really had not had any other option. In youth he had desired more than anything else a career of putting things into words, and the only writing jobs available were with newspapers, of which Larimont had precisely none. So, at age twenty-one, discouraged with a dreary job at the local feed and saddle store and convinced that if he didn't leave then he never would, John had packed up, boarded the train, and headed away from Larimont, leaving behind his widower father, William Kenton, a man known all over Larimont as Bill.

Bill Kenton was a longtime clerk at the Larimont Bank, and was in the eyes of the townsfolk as much a fixture at the institution as was the heavy oaken cage behind which he stood to do his work. John was sure that news of Bill Kenton's death must have stunned the whole town, just as it had stunned him. The idea of Bill Kenton being dead and gone was something that would take a long time to sink in.

As the buggy rolled along toward the Donaho Hotel at the far end of the street, John glanced over at Victoria Rivers's face. He could still see a faint look of sadness that showed most clearly in the mistiness of her eyes and the downturn of the corners of her mouth. As John looked at her he felt a great wave of appreciation for the woman who had brightened his father's last years. It had kept Bill Kenton from growing old, and Victoria, too, John supposed. Even now, just days after her beloved's death, she seemed five years older than she had looked six months earlier, when John had last seen her.

Victoria Rivers had done a lot for his father. But not even she had been able to spare him from untimely death, not when his house burned like a furnace around him in the night and killed him before he could hope to get out.

"Victoria?"

"Yes?"

"I want to know all about my father's death. Everything. I know it isn't easy for you to talk about, but I feel I should know exactly what happened."

"Yes, you should, John. And you will—just as soon as we can be alone to talk about it. I'll tell you everything I can then."

"I can't quit thinking about it, Victoria. Such a horrible, absurd accident . . . "

"That's the rub, John. It wasn't an accident."

"What?"

"Your father's death was no accident. But let's not discuss it here, all right? We'll get you a room, and then we can talk there, where it's quiet, where no one will hear."

John, shaken, pulled the buggy to a stop in front of the Donaho and walked stiffly into the lobby with his bag in hand. He nodded a wordless greeting at the hotel clerk who checked him in, then climbed the stairs to his room at the west end of the third floor. Victoria was at his side, as silent as he. All the while his mind turned over what she had said, and the implications it held.

John thrust key into lock and walked into a cold room with the musty smell of a place where windows are seldom opened. He tossed his bag onto the bed and walked across the room, where he opened the dirty window that overlooked the balcony above the street. For long seconds he stared blankly out to the dusty street and the people and wagons moving along it, then he said:

"It was murder. Is that what you were trying to tell me out there?"

"Yes, John. I'm certain of it. I couldn't be more certain."

13

John slapped the windowsill with both palms, then wheeled to face Victoria.

"God in heaven, why? And who?"

"I don't know. The marshal is investigating, but he's keeping an unusually quiet front about it. He won't discuss it with me, won't even confirm to me that Bill was murdered. Not that I need his confirmation. I know his death was no accident."

John breathed deeply, forcing himself to calm down. "Victoria, I want to know who killed my father. And mostly I want to know why. I want to look whoever did it in the eye and ask why anyone could possibly have a reason to kill a man like Bill Kenton."

John sat heavily on the side of the bed, his hands clasped in front of him, elbows on his knees. He stared at the wall for a time, then looked up at Victoria, whose face had taken on a hard, stoic look that masked whatever emotions she felt.

"How do you know he was murdered, Victoria? Didn't he die in the fire?"

"No. He was dead before the fire ever reached him. You remember Malcolm Weatherford, the undertaker? He told me, in secret and against the orders of the marshal, that your father had been shot in the head. There were no signs of powder burns around the wound, so it wasn't a close shot. That rules out suicide. And from the

14

looks of his throat it appeared he had inhaled no smoke. He was dead before that fire started."

"How could Malcolm tell all this?"

"Your father's body was not completely destroyed, despite what the marshal said. Malcolm told me your father was on his bed while the fire burned, and a beam above him collapsed and protected his upper body and head from the fire. The rest of him was . . . No need to talk about it. Like fire is, it was horrible, Malcolm said."

"Does the marshal have suspects?"

Victoria smiled very strangely. "Sometimes I think he's going to arrest *me*."

John was aghast. "You're not serious! How could he suspect you?"

"John, when it comes to killing a man like Bill Kenton, how could you suspect *anyone* in this town? Who lived here who didn't absolutely adore the man? Everyone knew him, everyone had nothing but good to say about him. So I suppose I'm as good a suspect as anyone else. After all, lovers sometimes kill one another."

John stood, tense and nervous. "It's preposterous, Victoria. I don't even like hearing you talk about it. And if the marshal is wasting time suspecting you, then the true killer is getting away free and clear. I'm going to have a talk with him, and—"

"I don't recommend that, John. Marshal

15

Roberts is a tight-lipped man about all this, and you know as well as I do how stubborn he is. He won't talk to you about it, I assure you. He has his own way of doing things, and sticks with it."

"But I have to do *something*!"

Victoria's expression grew stern. "John, listen to me. This isn't the time to grow hotheaded. If you follow your feelings instead of your reason right now, you'll only find trouble. If you want to get involved, at least do it in a cool, rational way. That's how to discover who killed Bill, not screaming in the face of a marshal. Think about it. You know I'm right."

John looked down and saw his hands trembling. Embarrassed, he stuck them in his pockets. "Yes. You're right. I'm sorry I burst out like that."

"It's easily forgiven at a time like this." She straightened suddenly. "I'm leaving for now. I'm very tired, and I want to get some rest tonight. It's starting to grow dusky outside, and I'd best be on my way. You needn't bother to ask to drive me—I'd rather be alone tonight. And you should keep to yourself, too. You have a lot to digest and accept. Get some rest before you talk to anyone."

"Very well."

"Good night, John. I'll see you in the morning. And do try to rest tonight."

John watched Victoria walk down the hallway and descend the stairs. He walked back into his room and closed the door, casting himself down on his bed while dark, saddening thoughts flitted through his mind like restless bats in a cavern.

Chapter Two

By the time John Kenton had washed and dressed the next morning and headed down the stairs with a mind toward breakfast at the Rose Café down the street, Victoria Rivers was downstairs in the lobby awaiting him. Outside, hitched to the rear of her buggy, was a beautiful chestnut mare, already saddled.

"You'll be needing a horse to get around," she said. "Keep her as long as you're in town."

John expressed his thanks to Victoria and walked over to the animal, admiring the graceful curve of its powerful flanks and the strength of its sleek neck. Victoria couldn't have provided him with a better horse.

"Have you had breakfast yet?" John asked.

"Yes, but I could enjoy a good cup of coffee—if you're going to the café anyway."

"I am, and I'm buying. Consider it rent for the horse. By the way, does she have a name?"

"Kate. Katherine, really, but if folks heard you calling your horse 'Katherine' you'd be laughed out of town."

John grinned. "Kate will do fine."

He took Victoria's arm. Together they walked down to the Rose Café, which had opened its doors about an hour before and was exuding a delicious aroma of fresh coffee and sizzling bacon.

John ordered a large meal, and Victoria ordered coffee, and as an afterthought, a fresh biscuit with molasses. Outside, the morning sun was beginning to warm the street, but the café, whose front doorway was shaded by a large cedar that grew alone right in the midst of the avenue, was cool and pleasantly dark.

Victoria's eyes took on a distant look as she sipped her coffee and stared out the open door into the street.

"You know, John, it's times like these that I can't convince myself Bill is gone. It's as if he should walk through the door at any moment, just like he always did. I wonder if I'll ever get over his death."

"I doubt you will. I discovered when my mother died that you never really get over a loss like that. You just get a little more used to it as time goes on. The pain is always there. You learn to ignore it and go on."

The breakfast ended quickly after that. The coming of morning had broken through John's gloom a little, but now the melancholy was returning, and the darkness of the café, which previously had seemed relaxing, was now stifling, filling him with the urge to get outside and into the open. Victoria left her coffee half unfinished, her biscuit three-fourths untouched. Sadness had overcome her, too.

The trip to the cemetery just beside the Presbyterian church came next. John had figured it would bother him, but when he looked at the fresh grave he felt no great shift of his emotions. But the sight set him to thinking again of the fact that his father had been murdered, and that he needed to make sure that justice came to whoever had taken his father's life.

"John! John Kenton!"

John turned to see who called him and saw, approaching at a half-walk, half-run, Lawrence Poteet, vice president of the Larimont Bank and a longtime associate of his father. Poteet, a stocky, red-faced man with round-lensed spectacles, slowed to a stop and extended his hand to John.

"Good to see you, John! Good to see you! But

I'm so sorry it has to be in circumstances like this. Terrible, terrible, your father's death. He was a good friend, John, a good friend. And a fine father to you."

"Indeed. Thank you. How have you been, Mr. Poteet?"

Poteet took off his spectacles and began wiping them with a linen pocket handerchief—a habit as much a part of him as his red face and small eyes. "I've been well enough myself, John. Of course, without your father, things have been difficult at the bank. He knew that place inside and out, and I never knew until he was gone just how much we relied on him. He'll be impossible to replace. I'm not sure the attempt will even be made."

"Hello, Lawrence," Victoria interjected.

The man's features turned even more red at Victoria's greeting, and John detected the hidden intent of her words. It was well known around Larimont that the old bachelor Lawrence Poteet had an eye for Victoria Rivers, but he was far too shy to ever make anyting more than halting conversation with her. Whenever he tried he always turned a fiery red—"blossomed out," John had heard one snide observer once call the phenomenon—and talked in a voice that let every one know his throat had gone as dry as Death Valley. Then out would come the handkerchief, wiping

22

furiously at the glasses, and soon the conversation would end as the nervous banker became too edgy to continue it. Victoria Rivers knew exactly the effect she had on the stocky little man, and was just mischievous enough to enjoy inflicting it.

"Well, hello, Victoria. Good to see you today."

"Why, thank you. Tell me, how is your poor old cat doing? I heard she was injured by a wagon."

"She passed away in suffering, sorry to say."

"Oh! How dreadful! Sad for you."

"Yes. Yes."

"Right. And how are people at the bank doing? Is Mr. Burrell well?"

"Fine. Yes. Indeed. Quite fine."

Victoria smiled warmly at Poteet, making his face turn even more of that famous blistering red. A following pause in the conversation was much enjoyed by John and Victoria, but Poteet was absolutely miserable, and suddenly found something fascinating about the tips of his shoes.

John couldn't watch the poor man suffer any more. Opening his mouth to break the silence, he found his words suddenly cut off by the noise of clattering hooves in the dirt as three riders raced around the corner of the dry goods store at the closest end of the street, heading out of town and into the Larimont Valley.

John glanced at Victoria and could tell by her expression that she had noted the same thing as he: The riders had been led by the county marshal, Drew Roberts, and they were moving in the general direction of the old William Kenton farm.

The old man had seen them coming before they were within a quarter mile of his shack, and even across that distance had sensed there was something out of the ordinary about the visit. He knew who it was—that buckskin horse of Drew Roberts's was an animal he knew well, having tended it many times in the livery.

He was drunk, as usual, and slightly embarrassed that in a few moments others would be seeing him in that condition. He knew he was foolish to even care, since everyone in town expected him to be drunk most of the time anyway, but he had been raised in a good home, and it just wasn't proper for a man with a good raising to let folks see him drunk if he could help it. Even a town drunk has his pride.

Outside, the marshal and his deputies had dismounted, and were approaching the shack. And with a sudden, disconcerting burst of comprehension, the old man realized that they were approaching under cover, darting from rocks to trees to the well to the woodpile—and their guns were drawn.

Now he was really scared, and confused. He had no idea why the marshal would be approaching his home like this. The palsylike trembling of his hands increased. He had been nervous ever since Bill Kenton's home had burned a few days earlier, only minutes after he had been there—and now this! He wished he could run out some back way and into the woods behind the shack, but there was no back way. He would have to face Marshal Roberts and his deputies. No way out.

"Scruff! Come out of there! This is Drew Roberts!"

Scruff Smithers's left eye narrowed as it always did when he was thinking. His drunken brain, scared through and through, blocked his very reasonable impulse to walk out the door with his hands up and find out just what Roberts wanted of him. No, there was something odd going on here, and he wasn't going to do anything without thinking it through first.

Scruff edged over to a nearby cabinet, opened it, and produced from inside a rusty but loaded Remington revolver.

He stared at the rickety handgun as his heartbeat grew faster and faster. The county marshal, outside with armed deputies . . . what could this mean?

A joke. A joke! It had to be. Drew Roberts was his friend, after all, and a man known to pull the occasional jest. Scruff grinned. That was it! Old Drew was trying to scare him, for fun.

Well, two could dance at that party! Maybe he could turn that little joke around, maybe scare Drew and his boys a bit in return.

"Scruff! You heard me! Come on out peaceful and nothing will happen. I need to talk to you!"

Scruff, blinking to clear the fog from his bleary eyes, staggered toward the door, gripping his pistol. He pushed the door open, stepped onto the porch, and raised the gun.

"Howdy, Drew! Come to roust out old Badman Smithers at last, have you? By granny, you ain't going to take me alive, no sir!"

And before he knew what his trembling hands had done, the old Remington roared and spit orange flame, the recoil knocking the pistol up to pound hard against his own forehead, knocking him down.

He hadn't meant to fire, not yet, and he had intended to shoot high. He'd forgotten about the hair trigger on this old pistol.

He had to make sure Drew understood the shot had been accidental. The old man tried to rise, but he'd stunned himself and his movements were slow. He pushed himself up on his right side, looking out fearfully to where Drew Roberts had just come to his feet, his pistol raised before him. The look on Roberts's face, Smithers noticed, was anything but playful.

In one horrible moment the old drunk real-ized that this wasn't a joke at all. Never had been. He raised his hand to gesture for the marshal not to fire, realizing only as he did it that the Remington was still gripped in that same hand.

Drew Roberts's pistol roared, and Scruff Smithers's body was kicked upward and back as a .44 slug tore though his chest, shattering a rib, tearing through his lungs, and exiting through his back. The world went black. He was vaguely conscious of another shot being fired, and it was as if a mountain's weight had crashed down onto his skull. By the time his next breath passed over his lips, he was dead.

Drew Roberts let his .44 slip back into its holster. He stood staring at the still, bloody fig-ure that lay half in, half out of the shack door-way, and slowly shook his head.

It was really too bad. He'd always liked old Scruff.

Chapter Three

The news traveled fast, making the rounds in Larimont seemingly moments after the town marshal and his two deputies arrived with Scruff Smithers's body draped over the back of his old mule. The body was wrapped in burlap sacks that had been dug up by the lawmen at Scruff's old shack, but they weren't sufficient to keep hidden the deep stain of blood on the limp corpse with its dangling arms. The marshal steadfastly refused to comment on what had happened; one of the deputies, though, a nervous, excitable greenhorn, let out a description of what had happened, and after that, telegraph lines couldn't have transmitted the story more quickly.

Poor Bill Kenton hadn't died by accident at all, the story went—Scruff Smithers had gone to his home, robbed him, then killed him. Somebody—nobody knew just who—had gone secretly to the marshal and reported that Scruff had been seen riding away from the Kenton house just minutes before the fire started, and the marshal and his men beat a path to Scruff's old shed as soon as they heard the news. But Scruff refused to surrender, coming out firing instead, and the lawmen had been forced to kill him. And sure enough, there in Scruff's pocket they had found Bill Kenton's watch. Sufficient proof that Scruff Smithers had killed poor old Bill and then burned down the house to cover the evidence.

It was unbelievable—Scruff Smithers just didn't seem the type to kill anybody. He was worthless, sure—and a drunk—but the story took a lot of telling before it really began to be believed.

And before long, people who at first had sworn Scruff Smithers couldn't possibly be guilty were talking in serious, covertly excited tones about different things they had heard the old drunk say throughout the years—things that at the time had seemed perfectly harmless, if perhaps a bit incoherent—but which in light of what had happened now seemed pregnant with diabolical intentions.

And in the midst of a Larimont buzzing with the sordid, unbelievable, and therefore delicious news, John Kenton sat in Marshal Roberts's office with a stony expression and an adamantly skeptical attitude.

Roberts, as usual, had little to say about the matter.

"You've already heard the tale, I guess, John. Scruff killed your father. It wasn't an accident, not a bit of it. Scruff killed him, and then wouldn't surrender to us. Shot at us! We had to drop him. No choice."

John shook his head. "Mr. Roberts, you and me have both known Scruff Smithers for years. Do you really think that he could do what you're saying? You know good and well he was a friend of my father. Scruff said a lot of times that he could always count on Bill Kenton when the rest of the town let him down. My father was almost a caretaker to Scruff—and he was a friend to him. Scruff wouldn't kill him. I know that."

Roberts's brows lowered ever so slightly. "Couldn't it be that it was your father's friendship with Scruff that led to this? Just imagine that your father tried just this once to shove old Scruff out. Maybe just one time he got tired of trying to help out the old bum. That could have made Scruff mad . . . mad enough to kill. And if Scruff was innocent, John, then why did he shoot at us? Hmm?"

John grew slightly sullen. "I don't know. But I don't think Scruff killed my father. I *know* he didn't."

Roberts sighed. "Then I'd appreciate it if you would fill me in on who did it. Me being the marshal and all, I'd think you might want me to know." The marshal made no effort to hide the sarcasm in his voice.

John stood up, twisting his hat in his hands. He thrust his hand up into his thick shock of sandy hair and ran his fingers through it like a man thinking hard about something he can't quite get a grasp on. Then he shook his head.

"Marshal, I don't know who killed my father, or why. I just can't believe Scruff could do it." He paused, his eyes clearing. "Just who put you on his trail, anyway?"

Drew Roberts tightened his thin lips into a hard line. "I can't tell you that, John. Official business."

John sneered slightly. "Just like everything else you don't want folks to know about, huh? Just call it official and shut up about it, right?"

Roberts showed no reaction to John's bitterness. John knew he was being a bit testy, but things had happened so fast and he was feeling so confused and bewildered by it all that he wasn't in the frame of mind to apologize. Roberts deserved some criticism, anyway, John figured. For a man on the public payroll, he was terribly closemouthed about things the public had a right to know.

"John, I've got work to do," the marshal said. "If there's nothing else, then why don't you just move on now? I think you'll realize that we have your father's killer after you've had time to get used to the notion. It seems to me it ought to make you happy."

"I don't see anything in all this business that could make anybody happy, Marshal. But we all look at things in our own way. So long."

John plopped his hat down on his head and headed for the door. He threw open the heavy oak door just in time to almost be barreled over by a tall, stout man who seemed in a terrible rush to get inside. John was pushed back and thrown off balance, managing to stay on his feet only by hanging on to the doorknob.

"Watch it!" he snapped, pulling himself upright again. The man who had rushed past him turned a pale face toward him and said nothing—but recognition cut off the torrent of invectives John was about to heap on him.

It was Alexander Layne, a neighbor of Bill Kenton and a man John had grown up nearby since his birth. And he was staring at John as if he were a total stranger.

"Alexander?" John queried in a tentative tone.

The husky man turned his back on John

quickly, pretending not to hear. Confused and strangely bothered, John ducked out the door and closed it behind him.

Strange, he thought to himself. But then, what wasn't strange anymore, with his father murdered and an old friend dead because—supposedly—he was the murderer?

When John told Victoria Rivers about Alexander Layne's strange behavior, she was as unable as he had been to give any good explanation for it.

"It's hard to imagine Alexander Layne not being friendly," she said. "Especially to an old friend like you . . . and at a time like this. Some folks are hard to figure—though I thought I knew Alexander better than that."

John's mind had already strayed back to Scruff Smithers.

"Victoria, do you believe that Scruff could have killed my father?"

Victoria's brows lifted, and she shook her head quietly.

"John . . . there's something about the whole thing that leaves me feeling like the mystery of Bill's death hasn't been solved yet. I've known Scruff for a long time, and though he was not an angel by any means, I'm convinced—at least I always have been—that he was harmless to everyone. Except himself."

"That's exactly how I feel, Victoria. Marshal Roberts may be ready to declare this case closed and let the whole thing slide, but I'm not. I've got to find out who really killed my father. My father's memory deserves that much."

"And maybe Scruff's memory, too," Victoria said. "Especially in light of this."

She reached over to a small end table beside her chair and pulled a letter out of the decorative oak box that normally served as a resting place for her spectacles.

"I got it today," she said. "It's from Sharon Bradley. Do you remember her?"

John knitted his brow. "Sharon Bradley . . . why, that's Scruff's sister's daughter, isn't it? The one who lived in Larimont until she was ten or so?"

"That's right. I've kept in touch with Sharon through the years, especially since her mother died. I did it partly out of friendship, partly because they wanted to always keep tabs on how Scruff was doing. They always called him Oliver—that's his real name . . . *was* his real name, you know. Sharon seems to have turned into quite a young lady. More and more through the last few months she's sounded concerned about her uncle, worrying about him, wishing she could get him away from Larimont, to someplace where he could get over his drinking. She was always worried about him . . . and now this." Victoria waved the letter.

"Get to the point, Victoria," John said.

"The point is that Sharon Bradley will be arriving in Larimont tomorrow about ten o'clock to meet her uncle Scruff and try to talk him into coming home with her, back to St. Paul. She doesn't know he's dead—there's no way she could. She's probably three quarters of the way through her trip now."

John winced. "I don't look forward to seeing her find out what happened to her uncle. And especially when she hears that he's being called a murderer by the law."

"There's nothing we can do about it, John. She'll be getting off that train tomorrow, and she'll be in for a big shock."

John had a sudden thought. "Victoria—the odds are that she'll want to clear her uncle's name, if she cared for him like you say she did."

"I'm sure she will."

John walked over to the window and pulled back the lace curtain. Down the dirt road he could see the steeple of the church and the corner of the cemetery. For a long moment he was quiet.

"Victoria, the law isn't going to be looking any further for my father's killer. They think they've got him. We both know they haven't.

36

My father was a good man, and he was killed. He deserves to have whatever vengeance he can, even after death, even if it has to come through his son finding his killer.

"And Scruff Smithers was a good man, too, in his way. He doesn't deserve to be called a killer. I owe it to him to clear this up, get him vindicated, though I know I can't bring him back.

"I've got to stay here until I can find out the truth. I've got to search out the killer and see him either dead or brought to justice."

Victoria nodded. "I understand. And I'll be at your side all the way. If you hadn't decided to do it, I would have taken the task on myself, alone. Somewhere, probably still in this town, there's a man who killed Bill Kenton in cold blood. I, for one, want to find him, and I'm glad to hear that you do too."

"And something tells me Sharon Bradley will have an interest in this as well," John said. "Maybe she'll be some help."

He turned back to the window. "But to me, this is almost a private thing. It's my search—the last thing I can ever do for my father."

It was almost sundown when John ran almost full-face into Alexander Layne outside the hardware store. As before, Layne appeared preoccupied, and seeing John standing before him seemed to almost frighten him.

"Hello, Alexander."

No answer but a nervous grunt.

"Is something bothering you? You didn't even say hello to me today."

Layne's eyes looked like those of a trapped animal. Abruptly he pushed past John, walking rapidly down the boardwalk.

"Alexander!"

The man turned, staring with a disturbed expression back at John.

"Was it you who told the marshal that you saw Scruff Smithers going out to my father's place the day he was killed?"

Alexander Layne's face went pale, and he turned and stalked away without a word.

Chapter Four

They buried Scruff Smithers the following morning, and folks came to the funeral to ogle the closed casket and hear the preacher expound about the wages of sin and the dangers of drink, about how Scruff Smithers had let himself become something less than human and how he had paid the price.

John sat on the back pew, feeling disgusted and knowing all the while that Scruff didn't deserve such a tirade. Probably the man who really killed his father was sitting in the sanctuary right now, feeling sure that his crime was going to be buried forever just as soon as they threw the dirt over Scruff's pine box.

John didn't go to the burial. It didn't seem

important, somehow. Instead he mounted up his horse and rode out to what remained of his father's house.

He found a hollow shell of a building that looked as if Sherman's army had marched through the middle of it. The rear walls were gone, as were most of the side walls, with only the front remaining in place, licked black with fire. The smell of smoldering wood ash still hung heavy on the farm, and the maple that had leaned over toward the front door was a blackened, dying relic of what it had been.

The house was like a thing dead; the farm was like a graveyard. John found himself growing increasingly depressed. He stood still for a long time at the front gate, staring blankly at the devastated remains of his boyhood home. Tears flowed down his cheeks for a full five minutes before he even realized he was crying.

He couldn't take it for long. He stayed at the farm for a little over an hour, then felt a strong desire to leave. He fetched Kate, who had wandered away toward a clump of thick clover east of the house, and began riding back toward town, resisting the impulse to turn and stare once more at the ghost of his past behind him.

As he rode he thought about Alexander

Layne. The man's behavior still bothered him, but he was increasingly sure he had hit on the reason for it when he had confronted him last night. It made sense, too. Alexander Layne's farm lay directly between Scruff's old shed and Bill Kenton's house, and Alexander Layne's front door and window looked right out toward the road. If anybody was likely to have seen Scruff riding away from the Kenton place, it would be Alexander Layne or one of his family.

Whether Scruff actually had been at the Kenton house before the fire was of little concern to John. He was sure that Scruff was innocent of his father's murder, and anyway, Scruff spent a lot of time at the Kenton house. As for the fact that Scruff had Bill Kenton's watch, John guessed that his father had given it to him, as he had given him many other little gifts through the years. Bill Kenton had always been a compassionate and generous man, especially with those who, like Scruff, were looked down on by most folks who considered themselves better.

John passed the Layne farm and resisted the temptation to stop and once again try to get something out of Alexander Layne. He saw no sign of life around the place. Probably Layne was out somewhere on his farm grounds. John rode on past the dirt road that led down to Layne's front door.

Up ahead he noticed a buggy rolling along. It was a fancy rig, shining and almost new, the kind that Larimont didn't see very often. Without making any attempt to catch up, he found himself gradually gaining on the slow-moving buggy, and before long he was along-side of it. He looked around and nodded at the driver. It was Frederick Burrell, president of the Larimont Bank, where his father had worked.

Burrell smiled at John, showing an even row of ivory teeth for an instant between his thin lips. Burrell was a tall man, not plump but slightly hefty and big-boned. Ladies consid-ered him handsome, John had heard, but he expected a good deal of the banker's attractive-ness lay in the fact that he had more money than any other man in Larimont.

Burrell was a nice enough fellow, and he had always paid Bill Kenton a good salary. John remembered that when he was very young, Burrell gave him a shiny five-cent piece every time he went into the bank. So the young man couldn't really figure out why he disliked the banker so. He always had, just as he had always hated spinach.

Shouting over the rumbling and creaking of the buggy, which was being shaken about a good deal because of the rough road, Burrell told John to pull over for a talk. John complied, not really anxious to talk to Burrell, but feeling there was no polite way out of it.

"John, there's no words that can describe the sorrow I feel about your father's death, especially with it being such an untimely and tragic passing. We miss him terribly at the bank."

"Thank you, sir. I appreciate the sympathy."

"You've been out at the farm, John? I saw it myself only a day ago—it was a painful thing to see. Of course, now that Scruff Smithers has paid the price for what he did, I guess—"

"Yes, sir," cut in John. He literally had to bite his lip to keep from bursting out at the tall banker. And he didn't want to hear any more talk against Scruff—not from Burrell, not from anybody.

"What brings you out this direction, Mr. Burrell?" John asked, trying to detour the conversation from the unpleasant direction it was taking.

"Visiting Alexander Layne and his wife," the banker said. "Or I should say, visiting Mrs. Layne. Alexander was out in the fields, and June and her mother were at the house. You know of Mrs. Layne's illness, don't you?"

"No," John answered. "I hadn't heard. What's wrong with her?"

"A bone problem, a stiffening of the joints," Burrell said. "She's bedridden, and has been for about six months now."

John frowned. He had heard nothing of Myrtle Layne's illness, and he was sincerely disturbed. Myrtle Layne was a woman he had liked since childhood.

"I hate to hear that," he said. "Is she in pain?"

"Comes and goes," said Burrell. "Lately it comes more often than it goes, I'm afraid. I try to visit her often—Alexander has always been a good friend, you know."

"Yes, sir."

Burrell picked up the traces and smiled thinly at John again. "I must be on my way, John—a lot to do today. Would you like to ride along? We can hitch your horse behind."

"No, thanks. I think I'll stop in and see the Laynes. It's been a while since I saw Mrs. Layne, anyway—at least a couple of years. So long."

John turned and started back toward the Layne house, while Burrell yanked the traces and began slowly rolling toward Larimont once more.

John felt a bit uncomfortable when he hitched his horse to the fence around Layne's yard. He knew that Alexander Layne for some reason didn't like to be near him now—his actions alone made that clear. But perhaps the Layne women would be different. And possibly he'd find out what was eating at Alexander.

June Layne answered John's knock. For a moment he was struck speechless, for the little brunette child that he had last seen maybe seven or eight years before had turned out to be a striking young woman.

Her eyes were wide and deeply brown, and her skin was fair and unblemished, though her cheeks were slightly sunburned. She had an honest, unpretentious look about her, and her figure was slim and very feminine. John couldn't help but notice that she had, as polite folks in Larimont put it, "filled out" very well.

"June? You remember me? I'm John Kenton."

"Yes . . . I remember you." June's voice evidenced no welcome. Her wide eyes had narrowed somewhat, cagily, and her expression was almost stern. Suddenly she didn't seem quite so pretty.

"I heard your mother is ill, June—I wanted to see her."

June shrugged and opened the door. It was the most reluctant welcome John had ever received.

John slipped off his hat and walked in. June closed the door and turned to wordlessly stare at John. Fingering his hat nervously, John asked how she had been.

"Fine."

An uncomfortable pause. "Good." John looked around. "Where is Mrs. Layne?"

"In the bedroom."

"May I see her?"

"Suit yourself."

John walked toward the bedroom, wondering if his reception from Myrtle Layne would be as cool as that her daughter had given him.

It wasn't. Myrtle Layne, her hair now gone almost completely white, greeted John warmly. Her fingers, John noted, were twisted and clawlike, and her frame appeared generally drawn. Her eyes showed that general weariness that marked a continual presence of pain.

"How are you feeling, Myrtle?" John asked. "I didn't know until today that you were sick. No one told me."

"Oh, I'm not really sick, John." She smiled. "Just getting old. That's what I tell myself, at least. Things could be a lot worse, you know. How's Victoria?"

"Fine. She's just fine. I take it you haven't seen her in a while?"

"I can't get out myself, and with us living out and away from town, I don't get many visitors. Occasionally some will come out for a visit, but it's all too often people are too busy. Good old Lawrence Poteet is good about stopping by, and occasionally Frederick Burrell does as well, though I haven't seen him in a couple of weeks."

"But, Myrtle, I just saw—" He stopped short, confused.

"Yes?"

"I . . . just feel surprised that you don't see more people. That's all."

Outside John heard the sound of the front door opening and shutting, and the sound of June's voice. A moment later, Alexander Layne's frame filled the bedroom door.

"Why are you here, John?"

"I'm just visiting your wife, Alexander. Is that a problem?"

"It might be. Don't you think you ought to give a man warning before you burst into his house?"

"I didn't burst in. Your daughter let me in. Now, will you tell me what's bothering you so much about me? I don't understand this."

"And neither do I, Alex," said Myrtle Layne. "John's a friend. You shouldn't talk so rough to him."

"Myrtle, you just hush. John made quite an accusation at me last night. I don't think I'm obligated to be kind to a man who would slander one of his oldest friends."

"Alexander, I'm sorry if I was out of line," John said. "I was just trying to understand why you were so cold toward me. I thought maybe, if it was you that accused Scruff, that my presence reminded you of all that had happened. I thought that was why you wouldn't talk to me."

"Did you hear that, Myrtle? He's accusing me of pointing fingers at folks—making me out to be something not much better than a murderer myself. I don't want him in this house."

"Don't worry," John spat out. "I'm leaving. I've done nothing to deserve this sort of treatment." He stalked out the bedroom door, June jumping aside as if she was afraid he would knock her over.

At the front door he turned. "But one thing I want you to know, Alexander—I'm convinced now that it was you who accused Scruff Smithers of killing my father. And I believe that you know as well as I do that he couldn't have done it." Then, slamming the door behind him, John stalked out.

And as he rode back toward town, he pondered why Myrtle Layne would tell him she hadn't seen Frederick Burrell, when the banker swore he had just visited her.

Like this whole confusing affair, it was an enigma he couldn't solve, and it bothered him.

A quarter mile from town, he heard the whistle of the train as it entered the valley. In a few moments Sharon Bradley would be in

Larimont and would be hearing that the uncle she came to rescue was dead and labeled a murderer. Just one more depressing detail in what was turning out to be a highly depressing day.

Chapter Five

Sharon Bradley took it rough.

John found her crying in Victoria's living room, with Victoria standing beside her, looking very guilty, as if having to tell this young lady about Scruff's death somehow made her partly responsible for it.

Sharon's face was tear-streaked and pale, and her hair was a mess from her having continually run her hands through it as she cried, but even in that condition she was a very beautiful girl, as John instantly noticed.

Sharon Bradley seemed somewhat embarrassed to meet John in her emotional state, and managed to stop crying, except for a few sniffles, as they exchanged their greetings.

After about an hour the tension in the air had lowered a little, and John relaxed. Sharon seemed to be getting over the initial shock of her uncle's death, and John noticed that he was beginning to enjoy her company. There were not all that many young women to whom John was easily attracted. A fellow had to take advantage of opportunities when they came his way, he decided.

John had grown up with Sharon until she moved east with her family while still a young girl. John had scarcely noticed her absence, since at that age he couldn't care less about some skinny girl who lived on the other side of Larimont. The only thing about Sharon Bradley that stood out in his mind from those early years was the fact that she always seemed to have a runny nose, and that she wore her auburn hair long and usually tied in pigtails.

Her hair was still long and auburn; the pigtails were gone. The runny nose was still there, but only because she had been crying.

She was a couple of years younger than John. But as he talked to her, he discovered to his delight that she was quite an intelligent young woman.

Victoria managed to coerce Sharon, through well-worded questions, into confessing that she had no serious courters. John looked at Victoria out of the corner of his eye. She hadn't fooled him. He knew for whose benefit that question had been.

Victoria warmed up some leftover potatoes and beans and set a good meal. John was ravenous and ate heartily, while Sharon picked at her food with an obvious lack of appetite. She was silent and apparently thoughtful for most of the meal, but at last began asking more questions about her uncle's death. John and Victoria answered them as best they could, and before long John was decribing the events of the morning.

"I can't figure out why Myrtle Layne would lie to me," John said. "Maybe she'd just forgotten Burrell's visit . . . but the man had been there only minutes before."

Victoria began picking up the plates and carrying them into the kitchen. On the last return trip she said, "John, have you considered that maybe it was Burrell, not Myrtle, who lied to you?"

John pondered that one. "It could be, I suppose. But why would Burrell lie?"

"Burrell . . . he's the bank president?" Sharon asked, trying to keep up.

"That's right," Victoria said. She paused, then spoke again.

"I'm not sure this is something I'm right to bring up, but I haven't fully trusted Frederick Burrell the last little while. Bill confided something to me about a week before his death. Nothing real definite—just that he was suspicious about Burrell over something or other. I think that it had something to do with that bank robbery a few months ago, because I know that at the time Bill was thinking a lot about the robbery. You remember that robbery, John? I assume Bill must have written to you about it."

"I haven't heard of it," Sharon cut in. "What happened?"

"It was a daytime robbery," Victoria said. "About noon, when the bank was just closing for lunch, three masked men pushed their way in and robbed the place of several thousand dollars. It was well-timed, happening just when the bank had a lot of cash on hand. Nothing really happened—the robbers took the cash and left. No one was hurt."

John chuckled. "Maybe Burrell robbed his own bank," he said.

Victoria shook her head. "I happen to know from talking with Bill that Burrell took a big loss in that robbery. He replaced the stolen money right out of his own pocket, just to keep the bank afloat. He wasn't benefited by it at all—that's why I never really understood why Bill was suspicious about him . . . assuming that suspicion had anything to do with the robbery, anyway."

"And it doesn't explain why Burrell would lie to me today, either," John said.

"John, you might want to talk to Lawrence Poteet sometime—very carefully and very discreetly. Bill said that Lawrence was also suspicious about Burrell in some way, though the two talked little about it. I know that Lawrence likes you, John. I think he would help you out if you approach him right. It could be that all of those suspicions and that bank robbery tie in somehow with your father's death."

"Could be. I think I will talk to Poteet . . . this afternoon."

John took off his hat as he walked into the Larimont Bank. Turning toward Lawrence Poteet's office, he immediately felt his foot step down on something that definitely wasn't floor.

That something was David Burrell's foot. The young man, about two years John's junior, was Frederick Burrell's youngest son. An older son, Michael, had left home years before, going east to work in a bank in St. Louis. The middle son, Edgar, had hung around Larimont, becoming known as town trash and causing a lot of embarrassment for his father and providing a lot of the cause for the drinking problem that had killed his mother.

David Burrell was his antithesis. Clean-cut and polite, the young man was never seen in any attire other than a tailored suit and tie, and his talk and general bearing were always stern and aloof. His reaction to John's clumsiness was in keeping with that image.

"Watch out, you oaf!" David bellowed, pushing John aside and striding out the door.

John would have been angry if he hadn't been so surprised. As it was, he merely watched the prim David Burrell stride haughtily away.

"I apologize for my son's behavior." John turned and saw Frederick Burrell smiling, extending his hand toward him. "David is sometimes less than tactful. I need to talk with him, I believe. Can I do something for you?"

"No, sir," John said. "I just wanted to have a word with Lawrence Poteet."

Burrell's eyes seemed to narrow slightly—or maybe it was just John's imagination. The banker's smile didn't fade.

"I'm afraid he's busy, John. Is it something I can help you with? If it's a banking matter . . . "

"It's not. And I think he's free—I just saw him walk into his office," John said, moving toward Poteet's office door. Burrell stared after him, his smile slowly fading.

"John—good to see you!" Poteet said as John walked into the little cubbyhole of an office that Burrell provided his vice president in the rear corner of the building. Musty and stacked with paper, the office—unlike Burrell's—was obviously that of a man who did a lot of work. Probably work that Burrell was supposed to do, John figured.

"Sit down, John. I just got some coffee off the stove in the back. Can I get you a cup?"

"No, thank you, Mr. Poteet. Just wanted to talk."

Poteet adjusted his glasses and squinted, puckering his thick lips at the same time. "Talk? What about?"

John looked out the open door of Poteet's office. Burrell had his back toward him and was shuffling papers in the teller's window, out of earshot.

"I wanted to talk about my father—and Mr. Burrell."

Poteet's ruddy face went pale, and his very official smile faded. His right hand, gripping his coffee cup, twitched convulsively, causing some of his coffee to splash over on his desktop.

"I don't understand."

"Mr. Poteet, I'm convinced my father's killing hasn't been solved. I think we both know that Scruff Smithers wasn't the sort of man to murder anyone. Which means that whoever did kill my father is still on the loose.

"You knew my father. You worked beside him, talked to him, and were a good friend. Maybe you know something about his last days, the days when he was bothered about something—Victoria told me that he was. She thinks it had something to do with the bank robbery a little while back."

Poteet shifted nervously in his seat. "John . . ." His voice was a whisper—a tremulous whisper at that. "John, this is hardly the time or the place to talk like that." He looked over John's shoulder, and John knew he was eyeing Burrell.

"Will you talk to me at all about it?" John asked. He knew he was pushing, and that he was making Poteet nervous. But this was a matter that deserved pushing, and he intended to get answers.

"I'm not sure I have anything to tell you—"

"Victoria told me that my father talked to her a while before he was killed, and that he said he was . . . curious, shall we say, about some details of Mr. Burrell's life. I don't know much more than that, but I think it had something to do with the bank robbery. And Victoria said that my father told her you had a few questions yourself. I want to find out about that. It's very important to me—more important than I can tell you."

Poteet glanced over John's shoulder once more, swallowing nervously. He raised his cup up and took a sip of coffee, and John noted that his hand was trembling.

"All right, John," he said quietly, looking down at his desktop. "But not here. Tonight, at my house. About eight o'clock. And try to be sure no one sees you."

John frowned. "You make this sound awfully secretive, Mr. Poteet. Do you know something that somebody doesn't want to get out?"

"I don't know anything," Poteet snapped quickly. Then his voice lowered. "But I . . . *wonder* about a few things. And maybe you have a right to know about it. Tonight, eight o'clock."

"I'll be there. Thank you, Mr. Poteet. Have a good day."

John walked out of Poteet's office, nodding at Burrell, who smiled back at him in a very hollow, artificial way. Then his eyes swung around and locked in on the nervous face of Lawrence Poteet, and the smile was gone.

Poteet delved into the papers on his desk, feeling sweat popping out on his brow, and hoping that Burrell couldn't tell how badly he was shaking.

Sharon Bradley felt a very unwomanly desire to curse. One wheel of Victoria's buggy, which she had allowed Sharon to borrow for a trip out to the Layne farm when the young lady had expressed an interest in seeing her old friend June Layne, was broken, thanks to an extra-large chuckhole right in the middle of the road. The buggy had gone as far as it would.

Sharon looked around her, wondering what to do. She considered trying to ride the horse back to town and getting John Kenton to come out and fix the buggy. But she was dressed in a long skirt—one of her best ones—and she didn't want to soil it. And riding with a long skirt was just about impossible anyway.

Only one thing to do. She would tie the horse in the woods nearby and hope that no one would steal it, and set out on foot along the old trail through the woods between the Layne farm and Larimont—assuming that old trail was still there. The Layne farm was still quite a ways off, and she didn't want to risk walking all the way there to get help. It wasn't the Laynes' responsibility, anyway. She would get John to help.

Unhitching the horse, she led it into the woodland and hitched it in a small clearing beside a gully that had a little murky water in the bottom. Then she lifted her skirts and began walking through the woods, trying to avoid snagging the fabric on the protruding branches around her.

The old trail was still there, just as it had been years before. It was a handy shortcut, about a quarter mile shorter than walking back along the road, and it was wide enough that she didn't have to worry about tearing her dress.

Walking along the old trail that she had often traveled in her girlhood brought back a lot of memories. And it was reassuring, in a way, to think that in all of the years since she had last seen Larimont, so many things were still the same. As she walked, she felt a kind of tingling, childish excitement.

She stopped in her tracks, suddenly holding her breath. Up ahead . . . had she seen someone moving?

She squinted through an opening in the brush alongside the trail. She *had* seen someone moving along toward the old Taylor shed—she had forgotten about that old hermit hideout—and it appeared to be a young man. She felt the impulse to hide. She couldn't tell who the young man was, with his back turned like it was. The only thing she could tell was that he was a fellow of average height, dressed in rather sloppy denims and a blue cotton shirt, with sandy hair hanging long and unkempt over his collar.

Forgetting about her dress's welfare, Sharon slipped as quietly as she could into the woods alongside the trail, settling down in a clump of young cedars.

It wasn't a moment too soon. Without warning, another figure came up the trail from behind. Sharon crouched down and held her breath, waiting for the figure to pass.

It was June Layne, walking alone. Sharon recognized her immediately, in spite of the fact that the last time she had seen her, both of them had been children. But those eyes were the same—there was no mistaking them.

Up ahead, the young man turned and looked down the trail. His face was vaguely familiar, but Sharon couldn't attach a name to it. When he saw June Layne, the young man waved and smiled. June walked toward him.

Sharon couldn't hear what they were saying—but the way he kissed June proved that the meeting was not accidental. And when the pair entered the old shed and closed the door behind them, Sharon realized that she had stumbled upon quite a clandestine affair indeed.

She slipped back onto the trail, moving swiftly in a crouch. She had lost the desire to walk back to town through the forest. When she greeted her old girlhood friend June, she didn't want it to be in such a clumsy situation as this. Some things were best kept secret.

She was already back on the main road again before she discovered that somehow she had managed to tear her dress. And what's more, her monogrammed hankerchief, one her mother had given her the past Christmas, was gone, probably hanging from some tree limb in the woods back along the trail.

It was too bad. That was her favorite hankerchief. Maybe she would get a chance to come back and look for it, sometime when secret lovers didn't occupy the woods.

Chapter Six

Lawrence Poteet's house stood on the northern side of Larimont, a stark and oppressive structure that was far too large for one man. Behind it stretched only stubble-covered fields, then wild meadows that in the summer bloomed in a profusion of color that stretched to the base of the mountains. But at night, with the few lights that Poteet kept lit shining out of dusty windows and the wide front door dark like a screaming mouth on the house's face, there was no trace of anything warm or inviting about the dwelling.

John hated to admit, it, but it scared him. Though the night was warm, he shivered a bit as he walked up toward the gaping front door.

He knocked with the brass ring hanging on the thick door, and imagined he could hear the echo ringing through the empty house—for Lawrence Poteet had little furniture, and little need for it. There was no answer, and John knocked again.

"Who is it?"

"John. John Kenton."

A pause. "You alone?"

"Just like we agreed."

John heard the banker fumbling with the bolt, then the door opened and Poteet hustled him inside, hurriedly shutting the door. John took off his hat and began to feel even more uncomfortable. Poteet was nervous in even routine situations, but not *this* nervous. John began to wonder what he was about to hear . . . and if he really wanted to hear it after all.

"Sit down, John," said Poteet. "Hang your hat here. Can I get you some coffee?"

"No, thanks, Mr. Poteet. I just had some supper. Where should I sit?"

"Here, anywhere. Just relax." Poteet took off his glasses and began wiping them. John found the man's nervousness to be contagious. He sat down in a stuffed maroon chair and immediately began fidgeting.

Poteet poured a glass of water from a pitcher on a low table in the middle of the room, and downed it rapidly. Then he sat down across from John in a stiff posture.

"I'm not sure it was good for me to have you here," he said. "It might not be a good thing for me to say the kind of things I've been thinking . . . "

"Mr. Poteet, I'm only interested in understanding why my father was killed. You can understand why I need to know, can't you? I'm a discreet person, and I won't betray any confidences. I want you to know that."

Poteet nodded. John noticed he was sweating. "That does make a difference, John. It does."

John sat back, waiting for Poteet to begin. He didn't, so John asked a question.

"Mr. Poteet, what kind of suspicions did you and my father have before he was killed? Was it connected with the bank robbery?"

Poteet nodded. "It was. The best thing I know to do is to tell you about the robbery.

"It happened maybe three and a half months ago, about midday. We were just closing down for lunch—had just let the last customer out— when three men, seemingly young, though it was hard to be sure, came in and drew pistols on us. They were masked with old flour sacks pulled over their heads, holes cut for eyes. I couldn't tell a thing about what they looked like.

"The bank had a lot of money in it right then,

and they got plenty of it. About seven thousand dollars, I believe. They tied all of us up and took off, locking the door. It took about a half hour for Bill to wiggle out of his ropes and turn us loose, then he took off and got the marshal. But it was too late then—they had gotten away, and nobody had seen anything that could serve as a clue about where they had gone.

"Well, we were all hot to get an investigation going—all of us except Burrell, at least. He seemed upset and angry, but he took it in stride, apparently, giving out little philosophical sayings about fate and so on. He answered a few questions for the marshal, but he didn't help any.

"Bill was the most anxious of any of us to find out who had robbed us, and for several days he was a regular firebrand, asking questions and so on. And every day Burrell got a little more close-mouthed, a little more discouraging to the idea of tracking down the robbers. He never came out and said anything about stopping the investigation, but he did come close to that, and did everything he could, it seemed, to throw blocks in the path of the marshal, and of Bill, who was conducting as much of an investigation as the marshal himself was. Eventually, the discouragement had its effect on Bill. All at once he stopped asking questions. He seemed glum, even depressed. He had little to say to anybody—

especially Burrell. I actually began to worry about him, but he shrugged off any friendly approaches from any of the bank staff. It was shortly after that that Bill was . . . was killed."

Poteet paused long enough for another drink of water. "I don't know what it was that affected Bill. It was as if he discovered something, or figured something out. And I'm sure it had something to do with Burrell."

"Is that all you know?" John probed. "Nothing more specific?"

"Not really . . . but in a way there is more. You see, it's not just the bank robbery that Burrell seemed to handle differently than he would have a few years back. It's the man in general, his attitude, his work as a whole. He's hardly ever at the bank anymore, and when he is he shuffles most of his work off onto me or some other bank staff member. He goes out for days without explanation, and will pack up and leave at a moment's notice and never tell where or why he's going. It's been that way for months now. I think—just conjecture, mind you—that maybe Burrell is seeing someone . . . a lady, if you take my meaning." Poteet dropped his head. He wasn't the kind of man to talk easily about such matters.

John shook his head. "Burrell having a love affair with someone? . . . That's hard to conceive, somehow. Who?"

"I have no idea. And honestly, I don't know it has a thing to do with the bank robbery or your father's death. All these things may be unrelated. But somehow I don't think so. Just a gut feeling, I guess. But I really believe there is some sort of connection."

John's voice was low. "Mr. Poteet . . . are you implying that Burrell had something to do with my father's death?"

Poteet jerked as if the question were a hammer blow. "No, John . . . surely not. Surely not. He couldn't do something like that. . . . " Poteet's voice trailed off into uncertainty, and John's stomach did a slow turn.

"Mr. Poteet, I can't believe that Burrell would do something like that, either. But I confess I've never liked the man, and certainly had no illusions that he is a saint. . . . But not even a man ten times as unlikeable as he is would be devil enough to kill my father."

"But *somebody* killed your father, John. And in a town this size, it was probably someone who knew him. Don't read too much into what I said about Burrell. I can't really believe he killed your father. . . . I can't believe that, and I won't. But somehow I believe that the *situations* are connected—Burrell's actions over the last few months, his attempts to play down the bank robbery while your father wanted to play it up, Bill's strange change of heart at the end, the way he acted toward Burrell in those last days, the way he expressed suspicions to me—similar suspicions to the ones I've expressed to you—all of those things seem to be tied in. Just how I can't say. But they are . . . and . . . "

John waited. "And what?"

"Perhaps I shouldn't say this . . . but I'm worried."

"About what?"

"About my own safety, John."

"What do you mean?"

Poteet looked away, looking disgusted at himself. "I've said too much, John. I shouldn't have said anything."

"Mr. Poteet, I need to know what you meant."

"I meant nothing. Forget it." The banker refused to look again at John. "I think you should go."

John stood reluctantly. "If that's what you want. Thank you, Mr. Poteet. Maybe we can talk later?"

"I doubt it. Please, John—just go."

John walked to the door and took his hat from the hat tree. He slipped it on his head and stepped out, looking back over his shoulder at Poteet, who was sitting as if in deep thought, staring at his shoes.

Out in the night John walked along until he

was on Larimont's main street, pondering the enigmatic things Poteet had told him. He was slightly disappointed at the vagueness of what the banker had said, but intrigued as well, and determined to delve further into the matter.

He could almost taste a solution to the mystery out there somewhere. He could feel it, sense that it was there. If only he could see into the right dark corner, turn over the right stone. He would find that answer.

And from now on his investigation would focus on one person—Frederick Burrell. It was there, he sensed, that the key to this mystery lay.

Lawrence Poteet was dreaming. Or at least he thought he was—in the half-drunken stupor into which he had drunk himself after John Kenton had left, it was hard to tell.

That noise—there it was again. And it was real, definitely no dream. Downstairs, a shuffling sort of noise, as if someone else were in the house.

Poteet felt his heart begin to race. The darkness suddenly became haunted and oppressive, the room intensely hot. His hand groped to his bedside and gripped the wooden handle of his Remington revolver.

Slowly he rose, cringing at the sound of the screaking floorboards at his feet. He moved silently to his bedroom door and, steeling his nerves, threw it open.

Only a dark hall out before him, and a staircase that faded into blackness at the foot of it, down in the living room where he had heard it . . . or him.

"Who's there?"

Silence. Silence and creeping fear.

"Who is it?"

Still no answer. But Poteet could feel a presence in the house with him. Stories of ghosts flooded in, and he began to tremble. Impossibilities suddenly became likelihoods.

Raising his pistol before him, he moved toward the staircase. After a long pause, he began creeping down the creaking steps, his heart hammering so forcefully that he could almost hear it.

"I've got a gun! I'll use it!" He was bothered by the weakness of his own voice.

He reached the base of the stairs and paused, looking all around. He saw the oil lamp on the table nearby, but was too scared to take time out to light it. He would have to put down his gun to do that . . . and when the light filled the room, whom, or what, might it reveal?

Trembling, he moved toward the front door. Maybe the noise had come from outside, just a wind in the trees, or a branch rubbing a window.

Slowly he unbolted and opened the door. The

night wind whipped in, rustling his nightshirt and raising chills up his back.

"Who's there?" he said softly.

No answer. He repeated the question, a little more loudly.

The gun was struck from his hand so swiftly, he couldn't even find the voice to scream. Something passed over his eyes, coming down from behind, and then his neck was being constricted, crushed by something rough and tight around it. Tighter, hurting . . .

The blackness rushed in, and he collapsed. Then a deeper blackness, and a numbness beyond anything he could ever imagine, and a sense of dying.

And then nothing.

Chapter Seven

John had tossed nervously all night. His mind had raced, refusing to stop, and he'd suffered with a vague, tense feeling that something was wrong somewhere. He finally settled down to sleep about four o'clock, and wound up dreaming he was in a railroad car that was bounding over the edge of a five-hundred-foot bridge, which caused him to jerk awake and wonder if he had yelled.

The darkness was making him nervous tonight, but he had too much pride to admit it to himself and light his bedside lamp. When morning finally seeped in through the gap between his curtains, he relaxed and drifted off to sleep.

He awoke a couple of hours later with the sun much higher and the noise of the street filtering through his slightly open window. There was the creaking of wagon wheels, the music of a woman's voice, the steady *whisk-whisk* of somebody sweeping off a boardwalk. He sat up and rubbed his eyes, yawning. He felt a bit foolish; in the sunlight the phantoms of the nighttime seemed terribly unreal.

John stretched his arms straight up above his head, then stood and rose on his toes, making his ankles pop, stretching his sleepy muscles. He walked over to the ceramic washbasin and splashed his face with water. Rubbing his whiskers, he pondered for a moment the idea of growing a beard, then shook his head. Some other time, maybe. He took a quick and painful cold shave.

John combed his hair and dressed in his last pair of clean trousers, making a mental note to ask Victoria to do some laundry for him today. He hated to push such a menial task onto her, but he would have more important things to occupy him.

John walked out into the hallway and turned the key in his lock, then headed downstairs with his mind on sizzling bacon and coffee. The lobby was empty except for the desk clerk, who was sitting with a cigar in his mouth and a month-old copy of a San Francisco newspaper in his hands. John walked past him, cutting through the heavy haze of cigar smoke and out the front door onto the boardwalk.

Leaning up against a porch column was a woman John didn't know. She was crying.

John slipped past her, looking at her out of the corner of his eye, pretending he didn't notice. He walked into the Rose Café and slipped into a seat at the table nearest the door. At the next table sat two men, both sipping coffee and talking in low voices. Without meaning to, John found himself listening to them, at first indifferently, then with sudden interest.

"Hard to believe he would do it. He never showed no inclinations to do such a thing, to my knowledge."

"Must have been awful lonely, more than people figured."

"They said he was hanging from the stair landing, like he'd tied a rope 'round his neck and the other end to the banister, then jumped. Snapped his neck bone like it was thin ice."

"Burrell's closed the bank, I reckon?"

"I reckon. Saw a wreath on the door a few minutes ago."

Elijah Smith, the owner and only waiter of the Rose Café, came over to John's table, coffeepot in hand. He poured steaming black liq-

uid into John's mug while John kept his eyes
fixed on the two men at the other table.

"Elijah, did something happen last night?"

"I reckon it did! Old Lawrence Poteet . . . he
hung hisself. With your pa gettin' killed and old
Lawrence dead, I reckon there must be some
kind of curse or somethin' on that bank. Yes,
sir—hung hisself."

John felt the color drain out of his face, and
suddenly he had no desire for coffee, food, or
human company. Without a word he rose and
stepped out the door, feeling weak. Elijah
Smith looked at him curiously as he left, then
shrugged and took John's coffee for himself.

John walked over to the livery stable and sat
down on a discarded wooden crate, feeling
almost ill. Lawrence Poteet, dead. And by his
own hand. That was hard to take in, especially
without warning like this.

Without warning . . .

John frowned down at his boot tips. What
was it that Lawrence Poteet had said, just
before he rushed John out last night? Something about feeling he wasn't safe . . .

John jerked to his feet. With a staunch assur-
ance he felt suddenly sure that Lawrence Poteet
hadn't hanged himself at all. For one thing, he
himself had given John a hint that he wasn't
safe, and second—and most important to someone who knew Lawrence Poteet for as long as

John had—Poteet would never, if he had a hundred years to try, be able to work up the nerve to snap his neck in two in such an unpleasant way as that man in the café had described. No way.

John entered the livery, saddled up Kate, and began riding at a good pace to Victoria's. He wanted to have a talk with her and Sharon, and quickly, for there was apparently a lot to talk about.

If Lawrence Poteet had been killed last night, it was possible, maybe likely, that it stemmed in some way from the fact that he had talked to John about Burrell. John mulled it over until his mind was a thunderstorm. When he rode past the lone tree in the middle of the main street, he felt a vague disgust for Frederick Burrell; by the time he dismounted in Victoria's front yard, he hated him. For it was clear to him now that if the evidence pointed toward any individual in Larimont, that individual was Burrell. Frederick Burrell, leading citizen, dignified banker . . . murderer?

John grunted a greeting to Victoria and pushed past her into the house, plopping down in a high-backed stuffed chair with a dark expression on his face. Sharon walked in from the kitchen. John could tell from her looks, and those of Victoria, that they had heard the news already.

"You know about Poteet. . . . Who told you?"

"Mrs. Chaffin next door. She came over right after breakfast with the news."

"Do you believe he hanged himself?"

Victoria looked noncommittal. "I don't know. Do you think he didn't?"

"I was over at his house last night, talking to him. He told me that he was suspicious of Burrell—he never spelled it out, just said he was suspicious. And he was scared, and said that he wasn't safe. I don't think he killed himself, Victoria—he couldn't have. He didn't have that kind of courage . . . and he was truly scared."

"This is horrible. . . . " Sharon sank down in a chair. "This is so terrible. I came and found that Bill Kenton was dead, that my own uncle was shot to death and labeled as a killer—and now *this*."

"Settle down, both of you," ordered Victoria. "It looks like there's something very dangerous and very underhanded going on around this town. We know that Bill was murdered, we know that Scruff never could have been the killer. And now it looks like Lawrence Poteet was murdered as well. Let's talk this over . . . put together what facts we have."

She pulled up a straight chair before John and motioned for Sharon to pull in closer. The group formed a triangle all around the low, central table in the room, and Victoria sat back and crossed her arms in a no-nonsense pose.

"We've got a few facts," she said. "Let's piece them together.

"First, we know that Bill was suspicious of Burrell in his last days of life. And we know that someone killed Bill—not Scruff Smithers, who could never have done such a thing. And now Lawrence Poteet is dead, probably murdered as well. And he, too, was suspicious of Burrell.

"All of that points toward a quite obvious suspect—Burrell himself. As for his motive, I have no idea. And whether he did the murder himself is something else we don't know. He could have hired it out."

"The motive is the big question," said John. "Why would he do it?"

"John, what did Poteet tell you about his suspicions toward Burrell? Bill never would describe his in any specific way."

"He said, for one thing, that he believed Burrell was having some sort of hidden love affair with some woman in this town," John said. "Such things as that can become motives for murder, you know."

Victoria was intrigued. "A love affair! That *is* interesting! Do you have any idea who?"

"Not a clue. I don't even know it's true," John said.

Victoria suddenly became thoughtful. "John,

you recall your visit with Myrtle Layne the other day, and how she said she hadn't seen Burrell in three weeks, and he claimed he had just visited her? Have you thought that out?"

"Victoria! You don't believe Myrtle Layne and Burrell—"

"Don't be ridiculous. But think . . . Myrtle Layne isn't the lying type—she probably was telling you the truth about not seeing Burrell. And obviously Burrell didn't see Alexander Layne, because he was away from the house. So who does that leave?"

John's eyes widened. "June Layne!"

Sharon gave out a sudden, involuntary yelp, and all eyes turned toward her.

"What is it, Sharon?" asked Victoria.

"I'm sorry. It's just that I . . . well, I know at least a little something about June Layne, something I didn't plan on telling anyone. I mean, it didn't seem to be something I should say . . . but I suppose I must.

"I saw June Layne yesterday, just before John came out and fixed the buggy wheel. I was walking through the woods, heading back for town, when I saw her meeting a man at the old Taylor shed. They went inside—I know I ran in on a secret lovers' meeting. It was obvious."

"Burrell?" John queried.

"No . . . a sandy-haired, sort of sloppy-looking fellow. Long hair."

82

Victoria's mouth dropped open. "Edgar Burrell!"

"That's sure who it sounds like," said John.

"Edgar Burrell?" Sharon said. "Isn't that Frederick Burrell's son?"

"It sure is," said John. "Do you realize what this means? It means that if Frederick Burrell is having a love affair with June Layne, then his own son is having an affair with the same woman. Now, doesn't *that* throw some interesting possibilities into the ring!"

"And it also establishes a tie between Burrell and the Layne family. Wasn't it Alexander Layne who accused my uncle of murdering your father?"

"Indeed he did," John said. He rose. "I think it's time I had a good, thorough talk with the marshal. To me, this is some interesting evidence. The law needs to take a very close look at Mr. Frederick Burrell, and waste no time about it."

An hour later, John was sitting in Drew Roberts's office, doing his best to keep from losing his temper as the marshal took what he'd given him and tore it to bits.

"Evidence? You don't have any," the lawman said around the butt of an unlighted cigar. "Think about what you're saying. You're accusing one of the most prominent men in this town, a man everyone respects and who has no criminal record of any sort, of being involved in some way in murder. Now, think this out, John. You've got Scruff Smithers's niece there willing to do anything at all to make her uncle look better. And let's face it—you've got yourself trying to prove some fool notion that somebody else killed your father when all the evidence points to Scruff. You've got an isolated event or two with the Burrell family—which may or may not be true, and even if they are don't show anything conclusive.

"John, I appreciate the fact that you're angry about what happened to your father, and the fact that because you're helpless to do anything about it you want to stir up something just to make yourself feel better. But this is an agency of law, and I can't just go out and make an accusation against a man like Frederick Burrell based on speculation.

"Like your notion that Lawrence Poteet was murdered—good Lord, man, the evidence all points toward suicide. So that's the way I have to treat it. I have to follow the evidence. Now, is there anything else I can do for you?"

There wasn't. So John left, feeling strangely abashed, and somehow sad—mostly because the marshal's words had halfway convinced him that perhaps he was wrong after all.

John stalked on out the door and into the

street, not even noticing the figure that sat sprawled on the bench on the front porch of the jail, a newspaper raised before him. As John walked down the street to where Kate was hitched in front of the gunsmith's shop, the paper lowered, and bleary, pale eyes stared after him.

Frederick Burrell peeled off two twenty-dollar bills and handed them to the man before him. Callused, nervous hands grasped the bills as if the man feared someone would get them before he could.

"Thank you, Jesse. I appreciate you keeping your ears open. You were right to come to me."

"You're welcome, Mr. Burrell. And I'll tell you anything else I hear. That I promise."

"You do and you'll get more of what I gave you," said Burrell with a smile. "It could be a lot more."

The man nodded and scurried toward the door. Burrell watched him head for the saloon, until a figure stepped into the open doorway, smiling at him.

"Edgar—what do you want?"

"Nothing, *Daddy*." The word had a contemptuous ring. "Just interested in what your little friend said."

"You've been eavesdropping? What in the hell makes you think that you can—"

"Sounds like John Kenton may be trouble for you, don't it, Daddy. Real trouble."

Frederick Burrell stood silently for a moment, stewing in anger at his son. Then, suddenly, he seemed to decide it wasn't worth it.

"Looks like it," he said. "Looks like it."

Silently, still grinning, Edgar Burrell slipped out through the door again. His father bit his lip, then moved over toward his office, where he shut the door behind him.

Chapter Eight

That night John ate supper alone in the Rose Café, pondering the things the marshal had said, looking hard at himself to see if all of his checking and suspicions and questions had come not from any real case against Frederick Burrell, but from some hidden desire to undo what he couldn't undo, to bring a man back from the dead.

Throughout the meal he really began to think that possibly that was it. It was when he stepped out in the moonlight and felt a cool breeze from the mountains whip against his face that he knew it wasn't.

There really *was* something here that was beyond the obvious. He wasn't digging in a dry well. Frederick Burrell had something to do with his father's death—he sensed it, he knew it. And no matter how long it took, he would prove it.

Back in a city many miles from here a job was awaiting his return, and a daily cycle of life was waiting to be resumed again.

It would just have to keep on waiting. There was a more important job to be done here, and it *would* be done.

John walked around the town, enjoying the feeling of his muscles stretching and his blood racing. The night air was delicious, like a refreshing drink, and the darkness was restful. The confidence he had lost earlier at the marshal's office began to return. Before John realized it, he had walked away the entire evening. Feeling pleasantly weary, he returned to the Donaho and climbed the stairs to his room.

He thrust the key in the lock and pushed open the door. He stepped inside, and sensed the other presence there only a moment before the universe came crashing in on his skull and he collapsed in a senseless heap on the floor.

Back in her room at Victoria's house, Sharon Bradley was dreaming about a cat.

It was an especially large cat, and a mad one. It was standing with its back arched high and its fanged mouth spitting, and it faced a man with claws for hands and the face of Frederick Burrell.

The cat leaped with a squall on the figure, and for a moment the world was a hurricane of fur and blood and wild screams, and then as suddenly the cat was gone and Sharon saw herself running through a dark forest with Burrell on her heels, and she was having trouble keeping ahead of him.

She awoke trembling. With a slight moan of horror she sat up in her bed, staring at the open door that led out into the upstairs hallway.

A figure was in the door—a large, black figure—and he wore a mask.

Sharon opened her mouth to scream, and hard though she tried, she found her voice was gone. And the figure was approaching her slowly, then with sudden, heart-stopping rapidity.

Rough hands grasped her wrists and forced her back down into the bed, and Sharon felt the roughness of the coarse cloth mask against her cheek. The weight of the man fell on her full force, knocking the breath from her and giving her her voice again.

She sent up a piercing, wailing scream, only to have a strong hand crush firmly and painfully down on her throat and cut off her voice.

"Give it up!" the figure growled in her ear in

a voice that sounded like a lizard's hiss. "Give it up!"

Sharon's hands flailed at her sides like those of a person drowning, her right hand digging uselessly into the sheet, her left hand groping about for something, anything. The kerosene lantern fell to the floor, the chimney shattering. Something else clacked to the floor beside it.

A knitting needle . . . one of the needles Sharon had been knitting with just before she went to sleep . . .

Her hand flailed wildly in search of that second needle, but she couldn't find it. The figure was crushing hard on top of her, and it began to sink in just what he was going to do. . . .

She found it. Her fist closed around the base of the needle, and with all the force that was in her she raised it high and drove the sharp point down.

The scream that erupted from the man atop her was agonized and horrible. The grip on her neck relaxed, and the figure pushed itself up. Sharon's hand slipped off the needle, and the figure rose to his feet, staggering toward the bedroom door, the needle thrust grotesquely into his back, rooted horribly deep.

The figure tried to reach behind as it walked, and its hands grasped the air in a vain effort to get hold of the needle. Like a fading nightmare the figure stumbled away toward the staircase, disappearing into the darkness. Sharon heard the sound of boots bumping roughly down the stairs, and the echo of groans through the house. Then came the noise of the front door opening, followed by silence.

She lay for a long moment in a strange paralysis, holding her breath. Then something broke inside her and she screamed, long and loud.

Sharon leaped from the bed and ran out onto the staircase. Her foot squished in something warm and slick ... blood. Ignoring it, she rushed down the stairs and into Victoria's room.

The moonlight streaming through the window revealed the older woman's form crumpled on the floor. Sharon gave a low, almost whispered cry, and moved to her side, almost afraid to touch her for fear she would find her lifeless.

"Victoria?"

She imagined she heard a faint moan. She touched Victoria's hand ... it was warm. Touching her wrist, she felt a pulse.

Carefully she rolled Victoria over onto her back. She looked around the room, and her eyes fastened on a glass of water on Victoria's bedside table. She scurried over and grabbed it, dipping her fingers into the water and bathing Victoria's brow.

After a long moment the woman's eyes fluttered open. In the moonlight Sharon could see the dull incomprehension in those eyes liven to terror as Victoria remembered. She looked up into Sharon's face like an insane woman, her lips pulled back to reveal gritted teeth, then relaxed as she recognized the young woman.

"Sharon . . . oh, God . . . "

"It's all right, Victoria. He's gone . . . and we're all right."

Sharon sensed rather than heard the figure that loomed suddenly in the bedroom doorway. All her strength drained from her like water out of a broken bottle, and she turned a pale face toward the doorway.

It was John. It took almost ten seconds for it to really sink in.

John struck a match and lit the lamp in the room, flooding it with a welcome light. Victoria managed to sit up, obviously groggy, and Sharon collapsed into a heap beside her, breathing hard.

"Are you both all right?" John asked. "Were you harmed?"

"I'm fine," answered Sharon in a very uncertain voice. "It's Victoria I'm worried about."

"I'm all right," Victoria said. "I took a good blow on the head, but I'm all right."

"Where did he go?" John said.

"He went out the front." Sharon paused. "I stabbed him."

"You what?"

"I stabbed him . . . with a knitting needle. In the back."

John didn't quite know what to say to that. He finally managed to stammer, "Did you kill him?"

"No. He went out. He might be dead now. I think I hurt him bad."

John shivered. "I can't believe it. Who would have thought it would come to this? But you know, this proves there's something to what we've been thinking. Somebody knows that we're checking into all of this, and they have something they want to keep hidden very badly. I was attacked, too, in my own room. Someone is trying hard to intimidate us."

Victoria was beginning to come out of her daze, and as she did, she grew shaky and frightened. John helped her to the bed, where she lay down, pressing her hand across her brow.

"Don't you think we ought to get the marshal?" Sharon asked.

"No!" snapped John. "We don't want him involved in this. What could we tell him? We have no proof, now that whoever-it-was is gone. And I don't trust the marshal now, besides."

Sharon thought for a moment. "There's blood on the stairs. I stepped in it."

"Yeah, but whose blood? The way Drew

Roberts feels about my notions and suspicions just now, I think he'd probably accuse us of setting the whole thing up just to make it look like whoever killed my father was still loose."

"John . . ."

"What is it?"

Victoria held up a torn sheet of paper. "Just now . . . I found this pinned to my gown."

John took the crumpled paper and unfolded it. On it were words scrawled crudely in splotched ink:

GIVE IT UP.

Chapter Nine

Drew Roberts grunted as he thrust the shovel deep into the soft earth atop the grave, and winced as a drop of sweat burned his eye. Tossing out the heap of red dirt to the graveside, he paused and pulled out a checkered handkerchief, with which he mopped his forehead.

Beside him stood J. W. Warner, caretaker of the church and cemetery. He leaned over the grave with an intent look on his face.

"Any sign of anything?"

"Not yet," replied the marshal.

It had been Warner that had called the marshal out of his bed this morning, excited and almost babbling. There was evidence, he said, of someone tampering with one of the graves in the cemetery—fresh dirt was heaped upon it, as if it had been dug into in the night.

Grave robbers, the caretaker theorized. A body had been stolen during the night.

Drew Roberts reserved his judgment until he saw the grave. Warner had told the truth. The grave had obviously been bothered. But the grave robber theory was doubtful, the marshal felt. Only one way to be sure, though. And so he had started digging.

After catching his breath, he once more thrust the shovel into the slightly moist dirt. Warner leaned even farther over the grave, watching impatiently.

The marshal's shovel struck something soft and resilient. Puzzled, he pulled back the shovel and dropped to his knees, digging in the dirt with his hands.

As the dirt was pushed back, something beneath it began to take a shape. Frowning, the marshal scraped away at the shape, removing more dirt. And in a moment, he jumped back involuntarily, shocked.

A face looked back at him. It was a pale face, frozen in an expression of pain. It took him a moment to recognize it, and before he could say the name Warner beat him to it.

"Sherman Horner," he whispered. "Sherman Horner, dead and buried!"

"He wasn't dead yesterday," Roberts said. "I

saw him myself about dusk. This happened last night."

He began digging further, clearing the dirt away from the body with both the shovel and his hands. In about ten minutes he had fully exposed the body, dressed in a checked blue shirt and faded work pants. The boots were gone.

"Help me pull him out, J. W.," the marshal said. Reluctantly, the caretaker, who had always been a little squeamish around dead bodies, stepped down into the open grave beside the marshal, trying to avoid stepping on the body.

The two men grasped the figure and pulled it upward. Dirt flaked off the corpse, whose mouth dropped open as the head tilted grotesquely back. After the body was free of the dirt the pair heaved it up and out of the grave, plopping it facedown on the grass. It was then that the deep red splotch of blood on the corpse's back became visible.

"Look at that!" exclaimed the marshal. "He's sure enough been stabbed!"

J. W. Warner wasn't looking. His face was pale and he was feeling quite weak, so he looked away from the body and down the road. He noticed a figure approaching, and elbowed the marshal.

"Somebody's coming."

The marshal turned and saw John Kenton

walking through the gateway of the cemetery fence. The lawman pursed his lips and muttered a very quiet curse.

"Marshal, I never thought I'd see you robbing a grave," John said. The derisive tone in his voice was apparent to the marshal, but it didn't bother him. He disliked John Kenton as much as the young man disliked him.

"Official business," said the marshal. "I'm going to have to ask you to leave."

"That's Sherman Horner, isn't it?" said John. "What killed him?"

"I asked you to leave," the marshal said. "And I'd advise you to get rid of that gun."

John glanced down at the Colt strapped to his hip. He had owned the gun for years, but this was the first time he had ever worn it. After the prior night's attack, he didn't plan to be without it, marshal's orders to the contrary or not.

"A lot of men in this town wear guns," John returned. "There's no law here that says I can't. It looks to me like Sherman has been stabbed . . . and I take it somebody buried him in this grave. That's real interesting. Sherman Horner . . . he's an old buddy of Edgar Burrell, isn't he?"

"I told you to leave, Kenton," the marshal snapped. "You'd best do it now, before I start wondering just how much you know about this body here."

"Sorry, Marshal," John said. "You've already convinced me that I don't know a thing about investigating crimes. You know, I think it's too bad old Scruff Smithers is dead . . . he would have been a handy peg to hang this murder on. Or do you think maybe it's suicide? Maybe Sherman stuck himself in the back and buried his own body."

John's sarcasm was eating at the marshal, and he stepped forward. "You'd best watch that mouth, Kenton. You're on the verge of getting locked up."

"Don't worry, Marshal. I'm leaving. I'll leave you to figure out what happened to old Sherman. But if you want a tip from an old armchair detective like me, talk to Edgar Burrell or Jerry Horner. I've got a feeling they'll have something to tell you about this."

John turned and stalked away, knowing that he should have kept his mouth shut. But the marshal irritated him, and he just hadn't been able to restrain himself. And besides, finding out just who it was who broke into Sharon and Victoria's house last night put a whole new twist on things.

The Horner brothers, Sherman and Jerry, had been friends of Edgar Burrell for many years. It was obvious that more than one person had been involved in last night's incident, for some second intruder had knocked out

John in his hotel room, and someone had buried Sherman's body.

It was, John felt sure, either Jerry Horner or Edgar Burrell. Most likely both.

Edgar Burrell. Jerry and Sherman Horner. Three men. Just like the three men who had robbed the Larimont Bank. It was intriguing. A whole new twist on this business was becoming apparent.

If Edgar Burrell had robbed his own father's bank, as unbelievable as that sounded, that would provide a good explanation for why Frederick Burrell had squelched an investigation of the robbery. If Burrell knew that his son was responsible, he might want to protect him.

But somehow that didn't sit quite right. Burrell had never been known as a man with a lot of affection for his oldest son. In fact, his low treatment of him, along with a few public slurs about Edgar's general "sorriness," as folks put, it, had made the rounds of Larimont gossip many times over the years. Burrell had often publicly stated that he figured Edgar would wind up either breaking rocks or stretching a rope. It didn't make sense that he would be protecting him.

But apart from that, there was yet another possibility that this opened up, and an even more important one.

It might not be Frederick Burrell who was

behind the deaths of Kenton and Lawrence Poteet. It might be the Horner brothers, or perhaps Edgar Burrell. Perhaps all of them together.

John was lurched out of his thought by a tall figure that stepped out before him from the door of the hardware store. It was Frederick Burrell, and his expression was stern.

"John, I need to talk with you," he said. "Now."

John looked at the banker with an expression of contempt. His own nerve was surprising him today.

"What's the problem?" he said.

"You're the problem—or rather, some of the things you've been saying. Let's go to my office and talk."

"No."

"I beg your pardon?"

"I said no. If you want to talk to me, then I'm here. Talk."

The banker's eyes snapped. "I'll not listen to impudence, you slanderer! I should have you thrashed for what you've said, accusing me to the marshal of being a murderer!"

John smiled coldly at the banker. "Now, I find that interesting. How do you manage to know what's told to the marshal in confidence?"

"Voices carry past closed doors—especially through open windows. You were overheard by a friend of mine, and I've got plenty of friends in this town. I'm afraid you might find yourself in a state of isolation here if you persist in spreading slanderous rumors."

"I'll persist in investigating the death of my father, and of Lawrence Poteet, sir," John replied. "And I'll do it no matter what the cost to myself. If you're innocent, you have nothing to fear. But if you're guilty, then I'll find you out."

Burrell was silent for a moment. "I can see that there is no point in continuing this conversation. You're mad. Literally mad."

Burrell pushed John aside and walked past him. A few steps down the boardwalk, he turned. "And as for the death of Lawrence Poteet, everyone knows that it was suicide."

"Oh, really? Like my father's suicide? That's what some said at first, you know."

"So I heard." Burrell turned again and walked away. John watched him, then continued on his walk, trying to piece together in his mind all he had found out so far.

"Old Pa really gave you a talking-to, didn't he, Kenton?" came a voice from an alley to John's right. John was slightly startled to hear the unexpected voice, and even more startled when he turned and looked into the face of Edgar Burrell.

Edgar was a sandy-haired, unkempt sort of

fellow, whose hair was always a shade too long and shaggy, looking as if he combed it mostly with his fingers. His face was rather broad and full in the jaws, and always present was a disarmingly friendly smile. His eyes were narrow and edged with slight wrinkles that were all the more prominent because of his smile, and his shoulders were broad and muscled—a phenomenon John couldn't account for, since Edgar Burrell was known to have never done a day's work in his life.

He was about John's age and height, and had a sort of easygoing, slump-shouldered bearing that made him look like the kind of fellow it would be easy to like. But John—and the rest of the population of Larimont who had known Edgar Burrell any length of time—knew that Edgar's true personality was not as pleasant as his appearance might initially indicate, and that in all the Larimont Valley there wasn't a lazier, more generally worthless bum than he was.

"Hello, Edgar."

"And hello to you, John Kenton. Long time no see. You want a beer?"

"It's a bit early. . . . "

"Hell, live a little! I'll buy."

John shrugged and accepted the offer, thinking to himself that he might uncover something informative by talking to Edgar Burrell.

Together they walked across the street to the

Larimont Saloon. The saloonkeeper, Ebenezer Drury, met them at the door with a full dustpan and a broom.

"Howdy, fellers. Sorry, ain't open yet."

"Eb, you'll let me in, won't you? I'll pay you extra for a good beer for me and my friend here. You remember John Kenton, don't you?"

Old Ebenezer squinted in John's face. "Well, I'll be! Good to see you, John. Sorry about your pa."

"Thank you, sir. But look, if you're not open for business, we can move on elsewhere."

"Nah, come on in," the other said. "I'll give you a beer in memory of your pa and all the business he never gave me. Never did see that man take a drink. A dry, dry man where liquor was concerned."

Edgar and John followed Ebenezer into the saloon and sat down at a table beside the front window, a red-checkered affair about halfway up, something like a stained-glass window. The light streamed in above, illuminating dust particles stirred up by Ebenezer's sweeping of moments before.

The saloonkeeper brought out two beers in heavy glass mugs and sat them before them on the table, then shuffled off to the rear stockroom, where he began banging around on some unknown but noisy task.

"Pretty little lady you been running around

with," said Edgar, grinning at John and taking a deep swallow of beer. He wound up with a foam mustache, which he didn't bother to wipe off.

John felt irked at Edgar's comment, and suddenly defensive of Sharon. He wasn't about to engage in a leering conversation.

"She's pretty. That's true."

"I reckon! What's her name? Sharon something?"

"That's right."

"Real fine-looking female, she is."

John stared coldly at Edgar. "Did you know Sherman Horner is dead?"

The smile didn't fade. "No . . . but then, I ain't surprised. Old Sherman, he probably tried to jump some old drunk or something . . . is that what happened? Ain't hung around with him in four or five years."

A lie. John knew it, too, for his father had made mention of Edgar and his two cohorts in one of the last letters he had written him. And it was obvious that Sherman Horner's death was no surprise to the grinning young roughneck.

John took a sip of his beer, and decided that beer for breakfast was an idea unlikely to catch on. Edgar sat grinning at him, eyes crinkling. John stared back at him with hardly a blink. As defiant as he felt this morning, there wasn't anybody who was likely to stare him down.

"John, old friend, let me be blunt with you. I hear that you're accusing my old man of killing your pa or something like that. How much would it be worth to you to shut up and cut off all this checking around you been doing?"

So this was it. A bribe. John found Edgar's open dishonesty somewhat refreshing. At least one knew where he stood with Edgar Burrell.

"Is there something worth keeping hidden that you don't want me to find?" asked John, mirroring Edgar's smile.

"Let's just say that nobody likes having his family probed into like you been doing," said Edgar. "I'm concerned that you don't go worrying my old man, you know. Fellow's got to look out for his own father, don't you see."

"Edgar, you intrigue me. And you sure make me feel certain I'm on the right track. As for your money, I don't want it."

Edgar Burrell reached into his pocket and pulled out a stack of bills, bound together by a paper wrapper plainly marked "Larimont Bank." John couldn't believe it.

Edgar read his expression of surprise, and apparently took it to be shock at the sight of so much money in one place, for he grinned even more broadly back at John.

"Sort of hard to resist when you see it lying out in front of you, ain't it?" he asked.

"Where did you get that money?" John asked.

"Got a rich daddy."

"Don't you keep your money in the bank? You always carry it around like that?"

"Don't trust banks."

"They can be robbed—right?"

"So I hear."

"Where did you get that band on the money?"

"Off my old man's desk. Listen—you want the money or not?"

"Did your father kill my father, or pay to have it done?"

"That's a hell of a question."

"I guess it is. How about an answer?"

Edgar reached out and retrieved his money, thrusting it back into his pocket. "You're a bigger fool than I took you for, Kenton. Terrible big fool."

John stood, making sure Edgar saw the Colt at his side. "No, Edgar. The fool is whoever killed my father—because one way or the other, I'm going to get him. You can bet on that."

John pushed out the door and into the sunlight. Inside, Edgar Burrell smiled and shook his head. He drained his beer, reached across the table, and took John's still-full mug and began drinking that beer as well, looking ever more thoughtful as he did.

It looked as if John Kenton was going to take a lot of convincing before he left Larimont. A lot of convincing.

Chapter Ten

"The journal!" John exclaimed. "Why didn't I think about the journal?"

John leaped up from the table in Victoria's dining room and tossed his napkin down on the plate, while Victoria stared at him with wide eyes and Sharon froze in place with a forkful of eggs halfway to her mouth.

"What are you talking about?" Victoria asked.

"The journal . . . my father always kept a journal," he said. "He wrote in it daily, like clockwork. It was a pretty secret thing, too. He never let me see it, and he always kept it locked in his safe."

Victoria began to understand. "And if it was

in the safe," she said, "then it might have survived the fire!"

"That's right," John stated. "And I'm willing to bet that it contains something of my father's suspicions about Burrell, maybe some things that we've overlooked or never known. It's worth checking into."

"But even if the safe is there, how can you get into it?" Sharon asked.

"Easy," said John. "My father gave me the combination years ago, so I could have access to it when he died. He kept his important papers there, or at least his more personal ones. The others are at the bank."

"I never realized that Bill kept a journal," said Victoria, looking wistful. "I wonder if he ever wrote anything about, well, about *me* in there?"

"He probably did," said John. "He really viewed that journal as a totally private thing, kind of the record of his most personal thoughts. You know, he made me promise once that when he died I would destroy it and never read it." John paused. "I guess I'll have no choice but to break that promise. I've got to. I won't read any more than I have to—to see if I can find some solution to this mystery in it. Then I'll destroy it, just like he would have wanted. I feel I owe him that much."

"Why would anyone write his thoughts down

every day, only to have them destroyed in the end?" Sharon asked. "I've always wondered about that. I don't think I could ever keep a journal—if I did I couldn't be honest about all I put in there."

"Me either," said John. "But my father was different. He never kept the journal until after my mother died. It was a replacement of sorts for her, I guess. Something he could share with in a way he didn't share at any other time. It filled a need for him."

"I can understand that," said Victoria. "When Daniel died, I felt terribly empty—like I could never talk to anyone again. Then I met Bill, and things were different. When your dearest loved one dies, you have a void inside. Bill filled that for me. Now he's gone, too."

"But maybe, in his journal, he's left part of himself behind," John said. "I'm going to my father's house. I'll let you know what I find."

Slipping his hat on his head, he left by way of the back door to the stable, where he saddled and mounted his horse. Kicking his heels into her flanks, he sent Kate down the road at a trot, her hooves kicking up dust behind.

He had moved into Victoria's house the night before, for after the attack it was obviously not safe for the two ladies to be staying alone. He didn't know how much safer things were with him there, but at least he felt more secure, both about them and about himself.

At his father's burned-out house, John dismounted and tethered his horse to a willow, then trotted toward the blackened structural shell. Skirting around the left side, he approached the portion of the house where his father had kept his safe.

It wasn't as badly burned as the other sections of the house, and a charred wall still stood there, for the most part intact. Stepping over the foundation, John stepped inside, his boot crunching ash beneath him.

He began to feel dismayed as he looked at the devastation all around him. The fire that had burned down this house had been a hot one—and although the safe surely must have made it through the blaze, there was no guarantee that the papers inside hadn't burned. What was more—and he hadn't thought of this before—the blaze might have melted the lock workings together, making it impossible to get into it without some sort of cutting equipment or dynamite.

Feeling less assured than before, John began moving aside burnt, fallen timbers and kicking away heaps of ashes. It took him only a little while to locate the safe, a blackened, rusty-looking relic of what it had been the last time he had seen it.

John knelt down before the safe, squinting as he peered at the combination lock. The paint had been seared off it, but he could still make out the numbers.

His fingers turned the dial. He frowned at the rough, jerky way the dial moved. Most likely the works of the lock had been damaged by heat.

In the forest about three hundred yards to the northwest, there was a rustling, almost slithering sound. John turned, but saw nothing except a movement in the branches of a young pine. Probably the wind or a dog. He resumed his work.

Breathless, he slowly lifted the handle of the safe door. With a rasping, creaking sound, it fought against him for a moment, then clicked completely up. John exhaled, smiling. The safe was open.

As he pulled open the door, a shower of ashes were sucked out around him. His heart fell. The papers inside were a black heap of useless ash.

He delved into the heap of black material, and his hand touched the edge of a book. Pulling it out, he recognized a now-seared copy of *Pilgrim's Progress* that his father always kept locked away, convinced that this particular edition was rare enough to be valuable. If it had been, it was no longer. John tossed it aside.

Reaching again into the pile of ashes, he felt a slimmer volume beneath the spot where the previous book had been. He pulled it out and dusted it off, and a smile broke across his face.

The journal. One corner burned off—the last few pages missing, but for the most part in one piece. He touched the cover, starting to open the book.

There was a sudden cracking sound from somewhere behind him, and immediately the safe rang out and John felt an uncomfortable concussion.

For a moment he sat staring almost stupidly at the safe door, wondering what in the devil had happened.

A shot. A shot had struck the safe door. . . .

Instinctively he rolled to the side just as another shot ripped above him and plunked into a blackened wall stud that poked out above the foundation. John was covered immediately with black, gummy ash. Diving behind a heap of rubble, he drew his Colt.

He had seen the powder smoke of that last shot. Someone was firing at him from the forest. Popping up like a gallery target, he fired a quick shot toward the spot from where the fire had come.

His bullet ripped harmlessly through the trees. Immediately two other quick shots rang out from some distance over, and John felt the lead sing past his ear. He dropped down again, teeth gritted. That had been far too close.

"Who are you?" he hollered. "What do you want?"

The only answer was silence. John figured that whoever was in the forest was probably moving again, trying to find a spot where he could get a better shot.

John looked around for better cover, struggling against panic. He saw the stones of the foundation sticking up behind him, and he realized the broken remains of the wall could serve as a protective screen.

Holding his breath, he leaped up, trying to move fast but feeling as if he was moving slowly, as in a dream. His foot slipped on the ashes beneath his boot, and he almost fell. Another shot blasted from the forest, and another bullet zinged overhead. John regained his footing and leaped over the wall, dropping to the dirt.

Quickly he replaced the spent cartridge in his gun with a new bullet. Then he peered carefully around the edge of the burnt wall.

He caught sight of something moving in the thickness of the brush, and he squeezed off a shot at it. Whether he hit it or not he couldn't tell.

Three rapid shots exploded from the forest, and the wood in the wall beside him snapped and spat out splinters and dust as the hot slugs tore through it. He dropped to his face on the ground, feeling utterly terrified for a few moments, then so angry that his fear was overcome.

He jerked upright and emptied four cylinders of his pistol toward the forest, squinting over the barrel with his lips pulled back in a tight snarl over his gritted teeth. And as he ducked again, he caught sight of a figure approaching from the opposite side of the farm, across the open area east of the road. The figure bore a rifle—and looked a lot like Alexander Layne.

John quickly reloaded, then rolled to the other side of the expanse of wall. Rising, he fired off a quick shot at the part of the forest he figured his enemy must have reached, and caught a glimpse at the same time, from the corner of his eye, of Alexander Layne dropping to his belly behind a boulder and leveling his rifle toward the forest where the hidden assailant was.

Toward the forest . . .

John realized that Alexander Layne hadn't come to help the hidden attacker but to defend John against him. John watched gratefully as Layne poured a withering, hot fusillade toward the forest. Judging from the steadiness of his fire, John figured that Layne, unlike himself, could see at whom he was firing.

John himself fired off two more shots. A sudden silence ensued, lasting about ten seconds. Then Layne's voice called.

"John Kenton! Are you all right?"

"Well enough! Who's shooting at me?"

"Don't know. Keep a sharp eye—I'm coming to join you!"

Layne leaped up and scurried, with his head low, toward the burned-out house. John expected to see more powder flashes from the forest, but none came. Layne dropped beside him, panting.

"Whew! I didn't know what would happen just then!"

Layne was different, John realized. Something had changed in his eyes, his speech, his manner, since the last time he'd seen him.

"What's going on here?" John asked. "Did you catch sight of whoever's out there?"

"Not enough to recognize him," Layne replied. "You know, I'm mighty glad I decided to follow you when I saw you ride past. Else I wouldn't have been close enough to help you out here."

John nodded. He looked carefully across the foundation wall toward the woods. Nothing.

After a long wait, Layne said, "Think he's gone?"

"Seems like it. Can't be sure, though."

"He might be moving around, trying to get behind us. We'd best get away from here."

"Where's your horse, Alexander?"

"On the other side of that rise yonder. I left him there when I heard the shots, and came on afoot."

"And my horse is over there," John said, pointing toward the spooked Kate, who pulled restlessly at her ties.

"We ought to make a break for it," said Layne. "A very careful break, with heads low. And if you would, I'd appreciate it if you'd give me a hitch over to my horse."

"I can do better than that," said John, and quickly explained a plan that had Layne nodding in agreement once he'd heard it.

John stuck the journal under his arm and held it tightly against his body. Together he and Layne came to their feet and darted around the edge of the house toward John's horse. No shots came from the woods. They reached the horse, and John quickly unhitched her.

He leaped astride the saddle with the dexterity of a Wild West showman, while Layne stayed on the ground, keeping the horse between himself and the woods. John sagged his body sideways, Indian-style, and kept as much of himself shielded by Kate's body as he could. He set Kate into a slow trot, praying the saddle cinch, and his straining legs, would hold.

Still no gunfire. Layne and John traveled,

John swung to the right from his saddle and Layne keeping pace on foot, over the top of a gentle swell of land to the northeast, until they reached Layne's horse and were out of sight and range of whoever had fired from the forest. All was silent.

John pulled himself upright in the saddle and let out a long, low sigh.

"He's gone now, whoever he was," Layne said. "I suppose he didn't like the odds of two against one." Layne mounted. "What were you doing at the house, John?"

John hesitated, still unsure even after what had just happened that he could trust Layne.

Layne read his suspicions. "Don't worry, John. Things are different now. I'm not going to run and hide from you anymore. Not for any reason, or any person. You can trust me."

John paused, then decided that indeed he would trust Layne. "I was looking for my father's journal," he said, "hoping I could find something in it to give me a clue about . . . all of this."

"And did you find it?"

John pulled the book from beneath his arm and displayed it to Layne.

Layne looked at it and nodded. "Come to my place. Nobody will bother you there, and you can look it over. Do you trust me?"

John thought it over one last time. "I trust you," he said.

Chapter Eleven

June Layne met John and her father at the door. The look she gave the pair was peculiar. But she said nothing as the two men brushed past her and entered a spare room, pulling the door shut after them.

Layne motioned John to a chair and pulled up one for himself. John looked at Alexander Layne uncertainly, wondering again if he should really trust a man who had acted so strangely before.

"I know," Layne said, noticing John's look. "You want me to explain myself. Well, I suppose you have a right to that."

"Alexander, we've been friends for years. Why did you treat me like you did before?"

Layne smiled sadly. "A bad conscience. Guilt."

"Over what?"

Layne's voice was low. "Scruff Smithers. It was me that told the marshal I saw Scruff Smithers riding out to your father's house before the murder and riding back just before the fire started."

"Was it true?"

"Yes. I did see him. But I know as well as you do that he didn't kill your father. He couldn't have. Not Scruff."

"So the marshal twisted what you'd said?"

"Not really. You see, I told him that I tried to call down Scruff, and that he rode by me like the devil . . . and that he looked scared to death."

"And that was a lie?"

"Yes."

"But why, Alexander?"

Layne suddenly sounded bitter. "Because of Frederick Burrell, that's why! Because he told me what to say about Scruff, and I said it!"

John felt a chill. "I still don't understand."

Layne looked at the floor. "Burrell holds the mortgage on my land, John. And I haven't done well over the last few years, and with my wife sick and all, it's been hard. Burrell has been easy on me, letting me get by with late payments. I owe him a lot. And the way he wanted to let me repay him was for me to get Scruff accused of killing your pa."

John was stunned, and for a moment he could only sit speechless. "So Burrell does have something to hide! And it must have something to do with my father's death, something he doesn't want brought out."

John glanced down at the journal. "Alexander, I'm glad you told me this. What you did to Scruff was wrong, but what you've done today is right. Now, let's see what my father wrote in here."

The door burst open. In the doorway stood Drew Roberts, staring coldly at John and Layne.

Roberts said, "Give me that book."

"Get out of my house!" shouted Layne, leaping up and causing the marshal to step back, his right hand edging an inch toward his side arm. "I won't have you storming into my home and taking property that isn't yours! This is still a free nation, you know! A citizen has his rights!"

"Shut up, Alexander," said the marshal. "I'm in my rights. I believe that book contains evidence pertinent to an open case."

"I won't give it to you," said John.

"You'll give it to me or I'll take it from you," the marshal said flatly. "You can have it either way you want it."

John gripped the journal tightly. "This is my personal property," he said. "I inherited it."

"Means nothing to me. Hand it over." Roberts's hand moved a little closer to his gun.

"Very strange that you showed up just now," John said. "Very strange that you know what this book is. You wouldn't happen to also know something about someone shooting at Alexander and me back near my father's house, would you?"

"Hand it over. I won't say it again."

"It was *you*, wasn't it! You're bought out by Burrell, just like some miserable hired gun hand! It was *you* who shot at us!"

Roberts lifted one brow. "That's a serious charge, Kenton. You'd best be careful about making it. Now, hand over that book!"

"He won't do it," Layne said. "And I believe he's right. It *was* you who shot at John from hiding, then took off like a coward when you suddenly had two instead of one against you! But you had just enough courage to follow us here. It all makes its own kind of sense."

Like lightning Roberts's pistol was out and leveled at John. "I'm tired of this babble. Give me that book now!"

There was no way out, and John knew it. Slowly, reluctantly, he handed the charred journal to the marshal. Just now he hated Roberts, hated him enough that he might have been able to kill him without much more provocation. But he wasn't a fool.

Roberts took the volume. "Now you stay clear of me," he warned. "Kenton, one more bit of trouble out of you, one more fool accusation against Mr. Burrell, and you'd best think about leaving Larimont quick. You understand me?"

John's gaze was stony. "If you've tied yourself to Burrell, then you'd best be the one to stay clear. I'll not back down until I know the truth about my father's death, whatever it takes."

Drew Roberts holstered his pistol and stalked away, saying no more. John watched him leave and felt the greatest frustration he'd ever known. He and Layne followed the marshal to the door, watched him go outside.

Roberts mounted his horse, then turned in the saddle and shouted back: "Layne! Mr. Burrell ain't going to be too happy with you for your part in this little turn of events. You know what I mean, I think."

John watched him until he disappeared, then turned to Layne. He was stunned to see the older man quietly crying.

"Alexander?"

"I've lost it all now," Layne said. "My land, my home . . . I'll lose it. Sure as the world, Burrell will take it all away."

John didn't know what to say. So he stood

silently, feeling uncomfortable and not a little guilty.

To the side, unnoticed, stood June Layne, her eyes wide and an expression of thoughtfulness on her face.

Dusk started high above the mountains, a faint grayness around the edges of the clouds that darkened to purplish black on the horizon. Then the shadows set in as the sun turned bloodred and sank toward the west, silhouetting the gap in the mountains through which the railroad led into the Larimont Valley. Then the darkness fell and lights winked on in the windows of Larimont, and enticing supper smells wafted out into the streets.

Sharon Bradley stood alone and nervous at the corner of the street and the alleyway that ran beside the jail. It was profoundly difficult to look nonchalant, and as she imagined that the short glances she received from the occasional passersby were suspicious ones, she struggled not to squirm.

She had cause to be edgy, for inside the dark jail John Kenton was hidden, digging through the marshal's desk like a thief after jewels. What he sought was his father's journal.

John had no way of knowing if the journal even existed anymore, for it was possible that the marshal had destroyed it as soon as he had taken it. But it was the only shot John had at getting back what he felt might be a valuable clue in solving the mystery that was coming to so obsess him, and he was willing to risk the consequences of breaking and entering a lawman's office and rifling his personal papers.

For an hour he and Sharon had stood hidden in an alley across the street, watching the jail until the marshal left. And then they had casually walked across the street, and John had gone around the back—leaving Sharon as a guard—and pried his way in through a back window.

And then he had started the hurried, silent searching in the office, looking in heaps of paper, in the cubbyholes of the beaten-up rolltop desk in the corner, and at last in the marshal's own desk. And the journal was so far nowhere to be found.

For a moment John wondered how Sharon was doing outside, and if she would be able to give him warning if the marshal approached. Then he yanked open another drawer and began shuffling through another heap of papers. He could hardly believe he was doing what he was.

The darkness outside was complete now. Sharon pulled her shawl around her shoulders to fight off the faint chill in the night breeze.

"Howdy, little lady."

Sharon jumped. The voice had come from nowhere. She looked around her, suddenly very frightened.

From the shadows a figure stepped out. It was Edgar Burrell. As usual, he was grinning— and drunk.

"Hello." Sharon was perturbed to hear her voice give a squeak a little like a rusty hinge.

"Mighty nice evenin'," Edgar said. Sharon could smell the whiskey on his breath as he drew closer. "A mite chilly, maybe."

"A little." Sharon wished she could run away.

"You know me, honey?"

The uninvited endearment scraped across Sharon's nerves, but she ignored it. "I think so."

"Well, tell me who I am, honey!" Then he laughed, and his alcohol-reeking breath forced Sharon to look away.

"You're Edgar Burrell."

"That's right! And you know, you're Sharon Bradley, the one who's been running around with that Kenton and saying all sorts of nasty things about my sweet ol' daddy. Now, why you doing that?"

"Please, sir . . . leave me alone." Sharon glanced at the jail. John still hadn't come out; he must be having trouble finding that journal. Sharon wished they hadn't tried to do this in the first place.

"Leave you alone?" he said in exaggerated shock. "My goodness! The little lady wants to run around town spreading lies about my daddy, and maybe even about me, and she wants me to leave her alone! Lord a'mighty!"

Sharon was beginning to feel a strong urge to run away, John or no John. But she couldn't do it. Sharon feared he would prance out innocently, not aware she had company, and incriminate himself and her right before Edgar Burrell.

"Mr. Burrell, please don't bother me. I'm not trying to give you any trouble. I'm waiting for someone here—please go."

"Waiting for someone?" he said. "You know, I think I'll just stand here and watch you. Like you do, y'know. Sort of peep at you."

Sharon had no idea what he was talking about, but his cryptic tone and manner worried her. "What do you mean?"

"Just this," he said, producing from his pocket a scarf, one that was terribly familiar to Sharon. It was monogrammed with the letters "S. B."

"That's mine!" she cried out, snatching at it. "Give it to me!"

"Yeah, it's yours," he said. "And you know where I found it, don't you! Out in the woods, near the old shed—"

"Give it here!"

"How long did you sit and watch me and June?" Edgar asked. "Not a very ladylike thing for a little prissy darlin' like you to do, was it?" He laughed in her face.

Sharon's hand flashed out and snatched away the scarf. Then she turned and began to stalk away, worried for her safety, praying that by deserting her post she wouldn't put John in a bad position.

Edgar Burrell grasped her shoulder, wheeling her around to face him.

"I don't want you to be asking any more questions," he said. "You or Kenton either. No more questions. You understand that? You'd best understand it . . . 'cause if you don't you might wind up in a hole like ol' Sherman Horner. Got it?"

With a rough shove he pushed her back. She staggered, but managed to keep her balance. Edgar Burrell walked rapidly away, fading into the darkness.

"Sharon?"

It was John's voice. He came around through the alley, a smile on his face. He had obviously not seen what had happened.

"I got it, Sharon! In the marshal's desk. Had to bust a lock. Now, let's get back to Victoria's and read it!"

Grasping her arm, he pulled her along beside him to where the buggy was parked a few hundred feet away. The pair climbed into the seat and took off down the dusty road into the night.

Chapter Twelve

Around a glowing kerosene lamp in Victoria's back room they gathered, drawing close together and talking in hushed voices, not because there was realistic danger of anyone outside their group hearing what was said, but simply because the covert nature of what they were doing made overcaution seem natural.

John opened up the charred volume and looked for a moment at the faces of Victoria and Sharon. Eagerness to hear what was written in the journal was evident in their expressions. John was eager too. Perhaps there would be an answer in this book.

The first pages of the journal were old, dating back over a year. John glanced at them hurriedly, occasionally catching an intriguing view of his father's thoughts on some subjects that he later had discussed with his son. Other entries were more routine, jottings about the weather, about a conversation held with some friend at the bank that day, about somebody down the road feeling ill. John wanted to linger at spots, for seeing his father's handwriting seemed to bring him closer, somehow. But he had promised that he would read no more than what pertained to the issue at hand, and he would keep that promise . . . he hoped. It wouldn't be easy.

"Do you see anything, John?" Sharon asked.

"Not yet. Nothing but regular daily stuff. . . . Wait a minute! He's writing about the robbery!"

"Will you read it? Aloud, I mean?" John glanced up at Victoria. He could see in her the same desire that he was having to suppress in himself—the urge to hear what the journal said as a means not only of gathering information but of bringing the memory of Bill Kenton a little more to life.

"All right. It's dated the day of the robbery."

John cleared his throat and began to read:

" 'Bank was robbed today. It was the first such experience of my life, terrifying. It's an unusual feeling to actually wonder if you're about to be shot by some nervous young masked scoundrel with a pistol. I'm frightened yet.

" 'They entered the bank—three of them— shortly after we closed for our midday break. All were masked, with sacks over their heads. They appeared young, but it was impossible to get a good look at them, the way they flitted around. And what's more, they forced us to lie on the floor, facedown, which made it difficult to watch them. That, I imagine, was their intention.

" 'I did catch sight of the eyes of one of them—it was a close look. He walked up to me and thrust his pistol right under my nose. The look of those eyes sticks with me, and I can't get rid of the idea that I know whom they belong to. But I just can't put my finger on it, can't figure it out. . . .

" 'I'm anxious to investigate this robbery. Mr. Burrell sent us home early today, supposedly to let us get over the shock. But he had the marshal in at the time I left, and I assume they were going over what evidence they had.' "

John flipped across the next few pages of the journal. The entries were still about the robbery, and of how Bill Kenton was growing restless to find the robbers. As John skimmed the writing, he read occasional excerpts aloud:

" 'Still no progress in the robbery investigation. Burrell seems strangely uncooperative, refusing to say much and offering virtually no encouragement in the matter. Strange. He stands a greater loss in this than any of us, yet he won't do anything about it. I must trust him. Surely he knows what he is doing.' "

John turned a few more pages, scanning them. A few pages later, he found another entry on the robbery.

" 'Burrell is covering something up. I'm sure of it. There is no other explanation for his reticence in this investigation. For days I've tried to talk to him about it, for I'm convinced that if we all put our heads together we stand a good chance of figuring this thing out. Poteet, too, has noticed Burrell's ways lately. He said as much to me today, though he didn't go into detail. I've determined to say no more to Burrell about the robbery. But I will watch him—as I have for months, since I've come to suspect he is having an illicit romance in this town. Wish I knew more. Crookedness in one area of his life might well lead to crookedness in another—like in the bank. And I want no part of that.

" 'That robber's eyes—they haunt me. I know him. But who is he? If only I could recall.' "

"This is fascinating!" said John. "I wonder if he ever figured it out."

Flipping through the pages as fast as his eyes

could scan the lines, he suddenly stopped. Aloud he read:

" 'Sherman Horner.

" 'The eyes that I saw were those of Sherman Horner. I have no doubt about it. And the possibilities that opens up are frightening.

" 'If Sherman Horner is guilty of the robbery, then it is tremendously likely his brother, too, is one of the robbers. And if those two are in on it, then surely Edgar Burrell is too, for that is a trio that is never separated.

" 'A son robbing his own father! It is hard for me to conceive. I'll go to the marshal with this information tomorrow.' "

John's eyes widened as he read that line. "He went to the marshal!" he exclaimed. "Victoria, Sharon—do you understand what that indicates? The marshal—who we know now is under Burrell's control—found out that my father had figured it all out. That means it surely got back to Burrell almost as soon as my father told the marshal. And if Burrell wanted badly enough to keep it all quiet, then he could have killed my father himself, hired someone to do it, or even had the marshal do it. Then Scruff was set up to take the blame. It hangs together."

"There are other possibilities, too, John," said Victoria. "What if Edgar Burrell or one of the Horners killed Bill? They may have gotten word that he suspected them of the robbery and then set out to shut him up. To me that makes more sense than saying Burrell did it. You see, we all know that Burrell wouldn't have a man killed just to protect Edgar. He doesn't care that much about him. But Edgar would protect himself, and we know that the Horner brothers were out to keep us from checking further. And he's the kind that would be capable of murder, I believe."

"There's more," cut in Sharon. "I ran into Edgar Burrell tonight. I haven't had a chance to tell you all until now, though."

Sharon outlined her encounter with the drunken young man outside the jail. When she was finished, John nodded.

"It does make sense—Edgar Burrell does seem to be a chief candidate for murderer in this case. But that leaves a few gaps—like why Frederick Burrell tried to squelch the investigation of the robbery, if in fact he wasn't trying to protect his son."

John picked up the journal again. "I'll see if there are any further clues in here."

He scanned the pages again. He noted a new sullenness in the writing. Some days had scarcely ten words as an entry, while others appeared written in a fast and angry hand, even though the subject matter was often innocuous. Bill Kenton's very writing was showing the growing dissatisfaction and anger that had marked his last days.

At last John's eyes fell on the last entry in the journal, written the day of the murder. Swallowing down the lump in his throat, he began to read.

" 'Same as usual at work today, though Burrell had nothing to say to me. Looks at me strangely when he thinks I don't see. I don't trust him.

" 'Saw Edgar Burrell today, and it was all I could do to look at him. I have no doubt of his guilt. Word has gotten around that I suspect his involvement in the robbery, somehow. The look he gave me was frightening.

" 'Feel depressed tonight. Scruff Smithers was by, and I gave him that gold watch he had long admired. I don't know just why I did it—it was a momentary impulse.

" 'I plan to retire early. I feel quite tired, and I want to—' "

"That's it," said John in a whisper. "That's all it says. It was as if he heard something, stopped in midsentence, and locked the journal away in the safe in a hurry."

"Something, or someone?" Sharon asked. "Looking at that journal may have been the last act of his life."

John closed the volume and pushed it away, a choking feeling making it hard to breathe.

And he was vaguely disappointed. The journal hadn't revealed the final clue that he had hoped it would. Unless it was that cryptic comment about Edgar Burrell.

Edgar Burrell. More and more John was beginning to think that Victoria was right. If anyone in this town had killed Bill Kenton, it seemed likely it was Edgar Burrell. It was all there—the motive, the ability, the character of a killer.

Victoria rose, breaking into John's thoughts. "I'll make some tea," she said quietly. "I think we could use it."

"I'll help," said Sharon. Quickly the pair slipped out of the room, leaving John alone to drop into thought once more.

Thought of one name, one face . . . Edgar Burrell.

Chapter Thirteen

Frederick Burrell was in a foul mood. He walked alone along the wide alleyway that was Larimont's version of a backstreet, his eyes cast downward and his forehead creased in thought.

Young Kenton was causing trouble for him. Just as his father had in the last weeks of his life. Burrell had friends in this town, and he knew the questions Kenton and that Bradley girl—hard to believe such a pretty thing was Scruff Smithers's niece—were asking around. And the hints of guilt they had been dropping didn't sit well with the banker. Something was going to have to be done. That was sure.

But what? Burrell had a reputation to

uphold. What could a man like him do to stop the rumors that were arising without incriminating himself?

It wasn't an easy question, and the more Burrell reflected on it the gloomier he became. He began walking more rapidly, his hands behind him. An old dog sauntered out across his path, and he kicked it away with a curse.

The figure that stepped from behind the next building startled him, and he reacted visibly. When he saw it was June Layne, he relaxed.

"Hello, June," he said, speaking low and looking around. "This is a surprise." He smiled. "A pleasant one, I might add."

"Stop it," she said. Burrell's smile faded. "I need to talk to you—seriously. And right now."

Burrell cocked his head. "Well, now! What's your problem?"

"It's not really mine," she said. "It's my father. And it concerns you, Fred."

"How so?"

"He's frightened, Fred. Frightened of you, and what you will do to him. Ever since Drew Roberts took that journal that Bill Kenton wrote, my father has been miserable, just waiting for you to foreclose as a punishment. I've come to ask you to not do that. Please."

Burrell smiled. "June . . . you know I don't want to do anything that would hurt you." He reached out to her, and she drew away. His expression chilled into cold stone.

"I'm serious about this," she said. "You mustn't do anything to hurt my father. I care about him."

"You're confusing me, June," he said. "Why do you think I would hurt your father? What does that journal have to do with me?"

"The fact that you know about that journal proves that it has to do with you, Fred," she said. "I know more than you think I do about your doings. I know that you're the one who had my father implicate Scruff Smithers, and that Drew Roberts is under your thumb. And that John Kenton and Sharon Bradley and all their questions have you worried."

Suddenly, without warning or change of expression, Burrell slapped June hard. She gasped and stepped back, staring at him in shock, her hand to her cheek.

"Don't you ever talk to me like that again, girl. I've treated you well, paid you well. And I've gone easy on your father and let him off dozens of times when he couldn't pay me. And half of that has been for your sake.

"But your father hasn't shown his gratitude very well, has he? Helping somebody like John Kenton, who wants nothing more than to see me hurt. What kind of man is that? And why should I do anything for him? Why should I be concerned about giving him extra time to make payments, when he obviously doesn't care what happens to me? Answer me that, June!"

June's eyes blurred with tears, and she sensed that she was losing. "Fred . . . I'm sorry. Please . . . don't hurt my father for what I've done. He needs help now, with Ma sick and all. . . ."

"I won't hurt your father, June. Not a bit. I'll just start treating him fairly under the law, as I could have done anytime up until now, and let him hurt himself. That's all it will take. Your father will destroy himself—he already destroyed himself, in fact, the minute that he crossed me."

June stood silent, tears streaming down her cheeks. She had failed. Not only failed, but perhaps made things worse.

"You'd best get home, June. Your poor old sick mother might need you. Good day." He turned and walked away, then turned again.

"There's only one thing that will make me change my mind about this," he said. "If John Kenton calls off his dogs and quits asking questions I don't like, if he quits trying to slander me and make me out a murderer, then perhaps I could be persuaded to go easy on Alexander. Just maybe. If you can work that out, then we'll see. We'll see."

He stalked off down the street and disappeared, leaving June alone with a feeling of hopelessness.

To persuade John Kenton to quit asking questions about his father's death—that was a hard bill of goods to deliver. Perhaps an impossible one.

Then the guilt came, flooding over her like a river pouring out of its banks, and she began to cry all the harder.

It was a hard decision. But once it was made, he felt he had no other choice.

Sooner or later, they were going to uncover the truth. It was obvious. No amount of persuasion had averted them yet, and there was only one other form of persuasion left. The hardest, the most final.

He slipped the last cartridge into the Winchester and hefted it to his shoulder, taking a practice aim in the mirror. Then he lowered the gun and stared at his reflection.

He would do it. Tonight, after dark. And then maybe all of this would stop.

It had to stop.

Sharon answered the knock on the door with the same caution she had used in all of her actions in the last few days. She swung open the doorway following a careful peek outside and looked with frank surprise at June Layne.

"June? I'm surprised to—I mean, why don't you come in? It's good to see you."

June walked through the doorway, smiling uncomfortably at Sharon. Sharon sensed a humbleness, even a fright, about June that had not been there before. Closing the door, she frowned slightly.

"Sit down, June. I'll get you a cup of tea. I just brewed some."

"Thank you, Sharon." June sat down near the cold fireplace. Victoria stepped into the kitchen doorway and looked out at Sharon's visitor, confusion evident in her expression. Then she stepped out into the room, wiping flour from her hands onto an apron. She smiled at June.

"Hello, dear. I haven't seen you in quite some time."

"Hello, Mrs. Rivers. Have you been well?"

"Fine." Victoria glanced at Sharon. This wasn't the same June Layne she had known for several years now—a brash, defiant young lady who rarely showed respect for her parents or any of their friends. This June Layne was quiet, humble, even scared.

Sharon went into the kitchen and returned a minute later with three cups of hot tea. She sat down near June and handed her a cup, then waited for the young lady to explain her visit.

"I have something to ask you," June said. "Something that's very important."

"Go on."

"I've come to ask you to stop."

"Stop? What do you mean?"

"Stop what you are doing. . . . Please, I don't mean to be pushy, and I'm not trying to tell you what to do. I'm just asking—and not for my sake, either. For my parents. You see, I . . . love them, no matter what some folks say about the way I act."

Sharon looked confused. "June, I'm not sure I understand what you mean."

June sipped her tea, and her hands were shaking. "I mean that I'm asking you, as honestly and as humbly as I know how, to stop asking questions about Bill Kenton's death. Quit trying to dig up anything about it. It's very important."

Sharon's countenance grew only the least bit stern. "Is there something that we shouldn't find out?" she asked.

"There's people, good people, who will be hurt," June answered. "I can't say much, but it will bring harm to my parents if you continue."

"Is it because your father helped John find the journal?" Sharon asked. "Is somebody trying to hurt him because of that?"

"Please don't ask me for specific details," said June, growing somewhat upset. Her hands were shaking so badly now that she had to put down her tea. "My father had nothing to do with what happened to John's father. I want you to know that. But there is somebody who will hurt him if you all keep on probing in wounds like you have. I don't want to see him hurt. Or my mother."

"Is it Burrell?"

There was a pause. "Please—I can't say anything right now. I just can't."

"And I can't stop asking questions. And neither can John. If he was here he'd tell you that, June. You see, my uncle was a good man, too, in his way. And he doesn't deserve to have his memory blotted with a smear like it has been. And Bill Kenton was a good man—and he certainly didn't deserve to die. That's why we *have* to ask questions. Do you understand?"

"Yes—yes, I understand. But I don't think *you* do! There's no justification for you both hurting innocent people just to find out what's past and done and unchangeable! Can't you see?"

"I can see that if a person is really innocent, then he shouldn't fear our questions. We don't want to hurt somebody that has done nothing. But we do want to see the guilty one uncovered, and justice done. And I can't go back on that."

June stood suddenly, upsetting her teacup. The night wind whistled in through the open window, suddenly chilling the room.

"I don't want to see my father put off his land, hurt by—"

Simultaneously with the blast of a rifle outside, the window shattered. June Layne fell back over her chair, landing facedown on the floor. She groaned once, tried to push herself up, then collapsed.

Suddenly weak, Sharon stood. She stared down at the form on the floor, then at the shattered window. She fainted just as Victoria's hand grasped her to pull her down to the floor, below the level of the windowsill and out of the line of any further fire from outside.

Slowly, a red pool formed around June Layne's body, and the only sound was the wind whistling through the empty window frame and the noise of rapidly retreating footsteps outside in the darkness.

Chapter Fourteen

"She wants to see you," the doctor said to Sharon. "She's insisting. Has been for some time."

Sharon had been trembling for two hours now. She didn't feel anywhere close to getting over it. Alexander Layne was in worse shape; he sat in the corner of his living room with his head in his hands. His wife sat beside him, all the more drawn and ill from the shock of it.

"Try to be strong when you talk to her," the doctor whispered in Sharon's ear as she moved toward the bedroom door. "That was a rifle slug she took, and it hurt her bad. I don't know how I'm going to tell Alexander, but I don't expect her to make it. But there's always the chance that she will—if she really believes she can. That's crucial. I want you to help her believe that, if you can."

"I'll try, Doctor," said Sharon. "I just hope I don't break down."

"If you feel that coming on, then get out of there," the doctor said. "Don't break down in front of her, whatever you do."

John caught Sharon's glance as she passed him. He smiled at her in a sad way, and she understood the meaning.

June Layne lay on her bed, propped up by pillows, her face pale, her eyes closed, with deep circles beneath them. Her chest was bandaged beneath her gown.

The doctor drew near June and bent down. His voice was gentle.

"You have a visitor, June. Sharon Bradley. Just like you asked."

June's eyes opened, fluttered, then focused on Sharon's face. She smiled.

"Thank you, Doctor. I need to talk to her . . . alone."

Sharon could tell from the strain in June's voice that she was in pain. Fighting back tears, she sat down in a cushioned chair beside the bed. She reached out and took June's hand.

"I'm so sorry, June. So sorry this happened."

Behind her the door closed as the doctor

stepped out of the room. June's face seemed to relax as she was left alone with Sharon.

"Sharon, I need to talk to you. I don't have much time, and—"

"Hush that kind of talk!" Sharon cut in. "You'll be fine."

"I'm dying, Sharon. I know I am. And there's some things I have to talk about before it happens. Things I have to set straight. Will you listen to me? You're the only one I can tell."

Sharon nodded tensely, not sure she really wanted to hear what June had to say. A deathbed confession of some sort . . . that was a frightening thing to have placed on her.

"I'll tell you as straight as I can what has been going on. What you do with this information is up to you . . . but I've got to get it out.

"I've been with Edgar Burrell a long time now. I mean that I've loved him, been close to him, been his lover. No one has known, except Edgar and me, and probably the Horner brothers. My mother and father, they've had no idea. They wouldn't approve of Edgar. He's not got a good reputation in this town—and I'll admit, he deserves that." There was a long pause. "And I know a lot of people frown on me too. And I deserve that. Far more than most would think.

"You see, Edgar had an idea, something we could do together that would make us both money. I knew then it was wrong, but Edgar persuaded me. I've never told anybody until now. . . .

"I've been . . . selling myself—you know what I mean—to Frederick Burrell for months now. It was Edgar's idea, though his father doesn't know it. I approached Frederick Burrell about it the first time, and he snatched up the offer. He's a perverse man, and an evil one, Sharon. But I went ahead with it, for Edgar, and for the money.

"Edgar and I would split the money that Frederick paid me.

"I know that it's wrong. I knew it all along—but I just couldn't stop, somehow. Edgar wanted me to do it, and I needed the money. And I think that my relationship with Fred was part of the reason he didn't foreclose on my father's farm long ago."

June had been staring at the ceiling throughout her talk, but now she looked over at Sharon.

"There. I've told you what's going on—what *has* been going on, I should say. But there are parts of this that even I don't know. And there's a connection to the death of John's father, I believe.

"You see, hardly more than a few hours ago Fred told me he was going to foreclose on my father's farm unless I could convince you to stop checking into Bill Kenton's death. That's why I came to you, asking what I did. It's obvious that Fred Burrell was involved in some way, directly or indirectly, with Bill Kenton's murder. Else why would he want to stop the investigation?"

Sharon nodded. "That's a good question, June. But do you think he's the one that shot you? And why would he do that?"

"I don't know who shot me," June answered. "But don't you see—they weren't after *me*."

Sharon felt a sudden chill. "What do you mean?"

"They were trying to kill you, Sharon. Somebody wanted you to stop the investigation—very badly. But they missed you and got me."

"Frederick Burrell?" Sharon whispered, her throat dry.

"I don't know," said June. "Why would he do a thing like that before he even gave me a chance to try to stop the investigation like he wanted me to? It could have been him, I guess, but I don't think it was."

Sharon forced herself to ask the question. "June, could it have been Edgar? He asked John once to stop the search for Bill Kenton's killer. He even offered him money. Do you think he could have—"

"I don't believe it," said June. "That's one

thing I won't let myself believe. I won't." She looked to the ceiling again.

"I'm sorry, June. I had to ask," Sharon said.

"I know."

Sharon ventured another question, noticing that June was beginning to appear tired. "June—why would Burrell try to blame Bill Kenton's murder on my uncle?"

"To divert the blame from himself. That's obvious. Your uncle was an easy out for him, and he used my father to implicate your uncle. Fred Burrell is like that—he uses people. He used me."

Sharon touched June's hand again. "Thank you for being so honest with me. I truly appreciate it. And don't worry—you'll be well soon. I know you will."

June looked unsmiling at Sharon. "I'll die," she said. "I'll die within hours. And the worst part of it is, I won't see Edgar before it happens. He won't come. They wouldn't let him in here if he did." The girl's eyes flooded with tears.

"I'm tired," she whispered. "I want to sleep."

"Goodbye, June," Sharon said, fighting back tears. "I'll come see you in the morning. I promise."

Then she was gone, getting out of the room as fast as she could, trying to hold back her weeping until she could get outside.

She pushed through the crowd in the living room and on out into the porch. Grasping a porch column to support herself, she cried like a child. John slipped out of the house and put his arm around her shoulder, feeling helpless and strangely bothered to see Sharon like this—bothered more than he could account for.

He looked into the yard for no particular reason, and his eyes locked onto the face of Edgar Burrell.

The young man stood beside a maple in the yard, staring blankly at John. The smile was gone. Edgar Burrell was changed. And beneath the blankness of his expression there was turmoil.

John sensed it all in a glance. Then Edgar Burrell turned away, mounted his horse, and rode off. John watched him until he was gone.

Shortly after midnight, the doctor walked out of June's room and informed her parents that she was dead.

Chapter Fifteen

"I've figured something out, I think," John said.

He had been sitting for several minutes with a cup of coffee in his hand and a thoughtful look in his eye. Victoria was seated, looking out a window, and Sharon seemed to be in sort of a weary trance. Since word had come of June's death, she'd hardly spoken.

John's words brought both her and Victoria around to reality again.

"What have you figured out?" Victoria asked.

"Burrell's motive for covering up the facts of the robbery," John said. "At least, I *think* I've figured it out."

"Let's hear it, then," Victoria said.

John took a sip of his coffee. "We've got a

new twist to the whole business considering the information that June gave to Sharon," he said. "It puts everything in quite a different light.

"Let's review what we know. First, we know that Edgar was fully aware of his father's involvement with June. I mean, it was Edgar who planned that whole thing. Now, imagine with me for a minute that Edgar goes to his father, the rich banker, the man of high standing in the community, and Edgar threatens to reveal his father's affair with June unless Burrell squelches any investigation of the bank robbery, because the bank robbery was done by Edgar himself, masked, with the Horner brothers."

Victoria was intrigued. "You may be onto something, John. It would mean that Burrell covered up his son's involvement in the robbery not to protect his *son*, but to protect himself, his reputation! It makes sense."

"It does," John said. "And it would mean that Burrell would have a strong motivation to get rid of my father when he began growing too curious and inquisitive about that robbery. Because if my father had managed to figure out that Edgar Burrell had been among the robbers, and if he made that public, then Edgar would have spilled the beans publicly about his father's love affair with June Layne. Burrell's reputation, his standing, would have been hopelessly ruined. So Burrell had to make sure that my father never revealed what he'd figured out.

"Or maybe there's a whole different angle. Maybe it wasn't Frederick Burrell at all. Edgar probably knew about my father's questions and suspicions, just like Frederick Burrell did. And he, as one of the bank robbers, had every reason to want my father to keep quiet, too. So it could have been Edgar who killed my father."

Victoria said, "And poor Lawrence Poteet was probably killed by the same person who killed your father. And now it seems that someone has tried to kill Sharon as well, probably to scare all of us away from digging any deeper." She paused. "It's a strange feeling, knowing that someone out there probably would be glad to see us all dead."

"Yes, and add to that the fact that the law here is corrupt and in Burrell's pocket, and you have to realize we have no protection beyond what we can provide for ourselves. We're in a tight and dangerous position, all of us. We'll have to closely watch our steps from here on."

"Yes," Victoria said. "Because we know that someone else already is."

"Let's consider what else we know," John said. "We know that it was Sherman Horner who attacked you and June and it was probably Jerry Horner who attacked me and knocked me cold. And we know that Edgar Burrell tried to bribe me out of investigating further. Take those things together, and you've got some pretty good evidence that Edgar and the Horner brothers had something to keep quiet. Pretty much a confirmation, in my opinion, that they definitely were the masked bank robbers."

Victoria asked, "Who do you think is more likely to have killed your father, John? Edgar, or his father?"

Sharon jumped in with her own answer before John could speak. "I believe it was Burrell. Because whoever shot Bill Kenton is almost certainly the same person who shot June, and Edgar would never have shot the very girl he loved."

"Maybe he didn't love her," John said. "Maybe he didn't care about her at all except as someone he could use to his own pleasure and benefit. Good lands, the man was actually encouraging her to sell herself, like some cheap trollop, to his own *father*! It's atrocious. How much could he have loved her if he was willing to let her do that? On the other hand, maybe June was right and that shot through the window wasn't intended for her. Maybe it was really intended for you, Sharon, or for Victoria. June might have been mistaken for one of you, and have been shot by pure mistake."

Victoria stood. "I think I'm going to go lie down awhile," she said. "I want to be sure I have the strength to make it through June's funeral. Right now I don't even feel like I have the strength to make it through the day."

When Victoria was gone, Sharon looked at John and said quietly, "It's all very dreadful, isn't it?"

John nodded. "Yes. It's all very dreadful."

The church was half filled a full hour before the funeral was scheduled to begin, and the closer the start grew, the faster the pews filled. Soon not a seat was left available, and John, Victoria, and Sharon were glad they had been among the early arrivals.

Sharon looked around the rapidly crowding room. "I suppose it adds a lot of curiosity to the situation when someone dies like poor June did."

"Morbidity," Victoria grumbled beneath her breath. "Pure morbidity! People will come any distance to gape at some person who has died in an unfortunate way. People love morbidity, and I despise the whole human race for it."

"It's why there's never a lack of a crowd at a good lynching," John said. "You know, if I could know for sure who killed my father, and if I could roust up a good lynch mob to take care of them for it, I'd welcome any crowd that wanted to watch the final disposition, morbid or not."

"In that case, John, so would I," Victoria said.

The preacher, a white-haired, humble little man with stooped shoulders and an eggshell voice that would be challenged indeed to be heard by a crowd as big as this one, shuffled to the pulpit to the accompaniment of a piano playing mournful hymns. The soft whispers and sounds of movement among the crowd slowly died away as he came to his place, leaned over the podium, and stared across the biggest crowd his church had seen in many a day.

"It's a sad thing," he began, "that often it is tragedy and death that bring us together in this way. How happy it would make me if many of you who have come here today to dwell on the sadness and sensation surrounding this untimely death would crowd these same pews on Sunday mornings to worship the Lord."

The crowd moved and fidgeted at this mild but unexpected scolding. Indeed many of them there hadn't even thought of entering the church doors in years and wouldn't have today if not for the way June Layne had died, and the wild, hot rumors that circulated about what might have been behind it.

"Nevertheless, I welcome you all," the old minister went on. "You are always welcome in the house of God, and in his kingdom as well, if only you'll accept his invitation." He cast his eyes down onto the closed pine coffin that lay on a table before the pulpit. "And in the kingdom of God there will be no more death, no more tears . . . no more staring eyes and wicked hearts that are stirred to passion only by that which is sensational and grim."

More shuffling, scooting, mumbling. This wasn't the kind of thing most had come to hear.

The preacher opened his Bible, cleared his throat, and began to read from the Gospel of John. The devout listened, while the nondevout stared at the coffin and wished it were open so they could get a good look at the corpse. These were the same people who had done their best to obtain all the gory details about the things the fire had done to the corpse of Bill Kenton, and whispered among themselves the lurid, gruesome details of Lawrence Poteet's hanging and the stabbing and mysterious burial of Sherman Horner.

The funeral dragged on, and John's mind began to wander. It fell into familiar paths, often walked these past days. He pondered angles, twists, possibilities, put together the facts this way and that, trying to see if something he hadn't noticed before presented itself.

He was startled, with the rest of the congregation, when the back door of the church burst open loudly as the preacher was about to begin a prayer. Turning his head, John was surprised to see Edgar Burrell standing in the doorway, disheveled, red-faced and red-eyed, shoulders slumped. He wore a heavy Colt pistol in a battered leather gunbelt slung loosely around his hips.

The preacher and congregation fell silent as Edgar simply stood there, obviously drunk, his bleary eyes sweeping over the assembly. His nose was crusted with old rheum and his face was wet with tears.

He stepped forward, walking down the center aisle toward the closed coffin.

"Young man," the preacher said. "I ask you, in the name of all that is holy, to respect the dignity of these rites."

"You can shut the hell up, old man," Edgar replied in a cracked voice. "You can just shut the hell up!"

John glanced at Victoria, then reached over and took Sharon's hand protectively.

Edgar Burrell reached the coffin. He stood

looking down at it, shoulders beginning to heave. He reeked of liquor; the smell reached every corner of the sanctuary.

The preacher stared down, looking as if he might faint at any moment.

Edgar Burrell wailed aloud, so suddenly that again the entire assembly was startled. He turned his head up, eyes toward the ceiling, fists balled and shaking in the air before him, and let out a long, bitter howl of a man deeply suffering. Then he fell to his knees, leaned forward, and rested his forehead against the side of the coffin.

"I'm sorry, June . . . I'm sorry . . . I didn't mean for it to be like this. . . . "

"Please," the preacher whispered. "Please . . . can't someone take him away?"

Men rose and went to Edgar's side. Gently they encouraged him to rise, to turn away. For a moment it seemed he would go along, but suddenly he swore loudly, shook them off, and stomped out of the church, still weeping.

The preacher stood there weakly after Edgar had gone, and remained silent because he simply did not know what to say.

At last his tired voice could be heard. "Perhaps," he said, "the best we can do just now is simply say a prayer, and lay this unfortunate young woman to rest as quickly as we can."

* * *

The burial was carried out in a tense atmosphere, everyone there fearing that Edgar might return and make a new and even worse spectacle of the affair. But he didn't return, and June Layne was given to the earth with at least a modicum of dignity remaining.

But Edgar wasn't through yet. A couple of hours after June Layne was buried, he showed up at the door of a local tavern. He was already quite drunk and belligerent, and infuriated when he found the tavern, which operated only in the late evening and night, hadn't opened its doors yet. He pounded and screamed and cursed at the doorway, until at last he received the attention of the barkeep, a quiet, easygoing fellow who lived in a room above the tavern.

The man tried to explain to Edgar that the tavern wouldn't open for another couple of hours, but Edgar would have none of it. He pushed his way in, and when the barkeep tried to restrain him, turned on the fellow and beat him almost senseless.

By now the matter had drawn attention, and someone called for the marshal. This display was too much for Drew Roberts to conveniently ignore, and Edgar Burrell found himself arrested and hauled off to the jail to calm down and sober up.

Not a soul in the town believed he would remain there long, nor see any official charges or legal retribution filed against him. He was, after all, Edgar Burrell, son of the man who ran Larimont, and Larimont's law.

Chapter Sixteen

John stood in the shadowed, recessed doorway, his face turned slightly to the right, his eyes cut to the left so he could watch the doorway of the jail and the marshal's office. He'd lingered there for about a half hour, and knew that he couldn't stay much longer without drawing someone's attention. But he had a feeling, just an intuition, that giving it a few minutes longer might pay off—and five minutes later, when the marshal's door opened and Drew Roberts emerged, hat on head, John smiled subtly. He watched Roberts stride down the street, heading toward the Larimont Bank. Checking in with Burrell, John assumed. Making sure the boss man understood why the marshal in his pocket had been forced to lock up his master's rampaging, drunken son, because to fail to do so would have destroyed any public credibility that his claim to be a fair and independent lawman might have had.

John waited until the marshal was well down the street before he stepped out of the doorway and walked casually toward the jailhouse. He was nervous, but also excited. Right now the jail was empty except for its lone prisoner, Edgar Burrell, and the marshal had left his office door unlocked.

John stepped onto the jail porch, resisted the urge to glance around and thereby make himself look suspicious, and opened the door. He stepped inside and closed the door behind him.

Sure enough, the place was empty. John took two or three deep breaths, calmed himself, and went to the door at the back of the office. The door opened onto the little hallway that ran between the three cagelike cells of the jail, one big one on the left, two smaller ones on the right.

John passed through the door and spotted Edgar Burrell at once. He lay in one of the smaller cells, curled up on the wood-slab bunk, his back toward John. John wondered if Edgar was sleeping. Some tense quality about him made him doubt it.

"Edgar."

The prisoner jerked, maybe surprised to hear a voice other than Drew Roberts's speaking to him. He pushed up, rolled around, faced John.

"I'll be damned," Edgar said. "I didn't figure to see you here."

"Quite a show you made at the funeral," John said. "And quite a job you did on that barman."

"Yeah. Wish I hadn't done that. Don't reckon he deserved it."

John looked closely at Edgar, who had a defeated, unargumentative manner just now, something seldom seen in Edgar's case. "You been crying, Edgar? Your eyes are a bit red-rimmed."

"I loved her, John. I loved that girl more than I ever loved anybody."

"If you loved her, how could you have had her do what she did, with your own *father*? She talked before she died. She told it all."

"I was wrong to let her do that. I know that now. But it just didn't seem to matter. Me and my old man, we've never had no affection for each other. I let June do that because it put money in her hand, and because it gave me something I could hold over the old man. To keep him under control, you know."

John hadn't expected to get this kind of unfettered honesty out of the usually cagey Edgar. "Tell me, then, was it you who robbed the Larimont Bank? With the Horner brothers?"

Edgar stared at him, then chuckled coldly, saying nothing.

John stared back. "It was. I can tell just by looking at you. Edgar Burrell, robber of his own father's bank! And your father knew it, too. But he couldn't allow the truth to be known, could he? Not only would it shame the great Burrell name to have it known his own flesh and blood had robbed the bank, it would also mean that you'd expose to all of Larimont that he and June were having a love affair. You set it up very cleverly, that I'll grant you. But you didn't anticipate somebody like me coming along, or somebody like Sharon Bradley. Somebody who wouldn't back down. And that's why you and the Horners paid those visits to me and Victoria and Sharon. Am I right?"

"Smart man, you are. Smarter than God! Now go off and leave me be. My head hurts."

"So I'm right, then. It really was you and the Horners who attacked me and two innocent women. But you didn't expect Sharon to have the presence of mind to stab a knitting needle into the back of her attacker. So once again, your plan didn't quite work out, did it? And Sherman Horner paid the price with his life."

"Smarter than God, yes sir. Why don't you go figure out somebody else's business and leave me be?"

"What about Lawrence Poteet, Edgar? Did you kill him, too?"

Edgar looked John in the eye and spoke with conviction. "No. No. That one, I swear, I had nothing to do with."

"Then who did?"

"I don't know. I swear I don't."

"What about June? Did you fire the shot that killed her?"

"No! God, no. I'd have never hurt her."

"But you might have if you didn't realize it was her. If you thought the woman you were aiming at through the window was Victoria Rivers or Sharon Bradley."

"I didn't do it, Kenton. I didn't shoot June! I swear!"

"Then why all the guilt at the funeral service? All the crying and moaning?"

"Because I knew that it was me who had put her in the position to get hurt. Because it was me who had gotten her involved with my father, and turned a good girl into something she never would have been if not for me. And in the end, it got her killed . . . but I swear, John Kenton, I *swear*, I didn't fire the shot that killed her!"

John gazed at Edgar, evaluating. If he was lying right now, he was doing a remarkably good job of it.

"One last question," John said, more softly.

"And this one is the most important of all. Did you kill my father, Edgar?"

"No. I vow to you, John, I didn't. I vow before God himself, it wasn't me."

"One of the Horners, then?"

"No. I don't believe so. I mean, if one of them had done it, I would know."

"I don't think I believe you. I think I'm looking at the murderer of my father right now."

"John, it wasn't me. I swear it."

"Why should I believe you?"

"Because I'm telling you the truth."

John locked a fierce gaze onto Edgar's face and held it in silence for a long time. When he spoke, his voice was low.

"You're in this jail right now because you got rowdy and hurt a man. Minor offense. You'll be out again soon. And when you are, I'll be waiting for you. I believe you killed my father, Edgar, and I'm going to make sure that you pay for that."

Edgar said, "I didn't do it, John. I didn't do it."

"Later, Edgar," John said. He turned on his heel and left.

John strode down the street in a cloud of rage, sure now that he had solved the grim mystery. Now what remained was to respond. There would be no help from the bought-off law in this town. He'd have to look higher than that. To the state, maybe.

Or to himself. One to one, man to man. That was the way to avenge Bill Kenton.

He looked up and saw Frederick and David Burrell walking toward him. He paused, letting them draw nearer, wondering if they were approaching him purposefully, or if their paths had just happened to cross.

"Hello, John," Frederick Burrell said coldly. David Burrell, pompous as ever, said nothing at all.

"You have something to say to me, Burrell?" John asked, making no attempt to avoid rudeness.

"I have nothing to say to you. We're heading to the jail to visit Edgar, and to get him out, if the marshal will allow."

"The marshal will do whatever you want, and you know it. I hope you do get Edgar out. I'm eager to spend some time with him."

The Burrells stared at him, seemingly trying to figure out what that last comment had meant.

"Good day to you, gentlemen," John said. "Enjoy your time with Edgar. While you still can."

He pushed between them, roughly, and continued on his way.

He knew he'd said too much. But he hadn't been able to squelch it. Edgar Burrell had killed his father, and he intended to kill Edgar in turn. And just now, he hardly cared who knew it, or what consequences it might bring later on, once it was done.

"It's him, Victoria. It's Edgar. I'm sure of it now." John spoke furiously, pacing back and forth in Victoria's sitting room as she and Sharon Bradley watched him and cast quick glances at each other. "I knew it while I talked to him. He killed my father."

"But John . . . how do you know?" Sharon asked. "I mean, what solid evidence do you have that—"

"Evidence? The evidence of my own intuitions!"

"Well, John, don't take offense at me saying this, but intuition and evidence are not quite the same thing. . . . "

"Listen to me, I know what I know. Maybe I can't prove it in the legal sense . . . but I know."

Victoria stood. "John, would you like some food, something to drink, maybe sit down and settle your mind a little?"

John frowned at her. "Settle my mind? What are you saying?"

"Just that you're overwrought. Your feelings are running ahead of your common sense."

He frowned even more deeply. "You don't believe me!"

"No, quite honestly, I think I do. I can't think of a more likely candidate to have killed Bill. But the fact remains that you still lack *proof*."

"And what good is proof except in a court of law? And what good is a court of law in Larimont, where Frederick Burrell has bought the law for himself?"

"Not entirely," Sharon suggested. "I mean, the marshal did lock up Edgar for beating that poor man."

"Well, he hardly had any choice about that! Edgar's violation was too flagrant for him just to let it pass. He has to keep up his front before the public eye, you know. But Edgar will be out before you know it. He probably already is. The other Burrells were on their way over to the jail to try to get him out when I came out."

"John, listen to me," Victoria said. "You're beginning to let all this wear away at you a little too much. You're going to let yourself get emotional, make mistakes. You need to rest, to think. I suggest you go back to your hotel for a while. Take a nap. See no one. And *calm down*! The last thing you want to do is run out of control, like some train leaping its tracks for going too fast. Do you understand what I'm saying?"

John fought back the impulse to be irritated at what Victoria said, because he knew she was right.

"I understand."

"Good. Of course, you're welcome to stay here, too. You can go lie down in the back bedroom, if you like. Take a nap."

"No, no. I'll go back to the hotel."

"May I send you some food?"

"I'll get something at the café later."

Victoria went to him and kissed his cheek. "Good. Rest and a cleared mind is what you need. Then we'll gather again and talk about how to gather solid proof against Edgar . . . not just intuitions."

John smiled at her. A wise woman, like a mother to him. He was glad she was around to keep him from losing his moorings.

He said his farewells, left the house, and walked toward the hotel.

Chapter Seventeen

Somewhere between Victoria's and the hotel, John grew caught up in a memory from childhood that arose at the sight of a long-legged pup that scampered to him from somewhere, played and bounced about his feet a few moments, then darted happily away down the street. It reminded him of a similar pup he'd picked up as a boy, only that pup had been injured in some manner, and homeless. He'd taken it in and raised it, with his father's permission and help. Old Toby. The dog had been his boon companion for almost a decade. He was buried now in an unmarked grave to the west of the black rubble that was all that remained of Bill Kenton's house.

John was mentally running through a field with Old Toby as he reached his room. His hand gripped the knob and he dug for a key, only to be surprised when the knob turned freely in his hand and the door opened, already unlocked.

John peered in cautiously, saw nothing amiss, stepped slowly inside, turned, and let out a gasp.

"Hello, John," David Burrell said to him. Edgar's dandified brother was seated very casually in a chair in the far corner of the room. "Glad you finally made it back. I was beginning to grow weary of waiting for you."

"What the devil are you doing in my room?"

"I told you. Waiting for you."

"How did you get in here? I left this door locked."

"Money is the key that opens all locks, John. I paid the hotel manager to let me in. Quite simple."

"You have no business here. Go away."

"Oh, John, John, don't start acting that way. Yes, I know I have no legal right to be here. Yes, I know you probably don't like me or any of my family. Yes, this is probably a bit frightening . . . but since I am here, can't we just talk for a moment? That's all I've come for."

John's heart was beginning to slow down a little. The shock of encountering someone in his room had sent it racing. But as he looked at David, he ceased to worry quite as much. The young man certainly wasn't acting threatening, and he'd never perceived the young swell as a dangerous type. Annoying and overbearing, maybe, but not dangerous.

"What do you want to talk about?" John asked tentatively.

David's manner changed in a barely perceptible way. He grew a touch less arrogant. "I want to talk about my family, and the terrible situations that have come up lately."

"The killings, you mean."

"Well . . . yes. That. And all the gossip and slander and so on. It's creating some . . . *problems* for the Burrell family."

"The Kenton family hasn't fared too well lately, either. My father was murdered, and a lot of effort has been made to make sure that no one asks too many questions about how it happened."

"Yes. I know. And I'm sorry about your father, John. I truly mean that. It was terrible that he died. He was a good man."

"Quite honestly, I'm surprised you even noticed. I've always perceived you, to be truthful, as totally wrapped up in yourself."

David smiled. "I probably deserve that. Yes . . . I suppose I do. I must admit, that I've always been a proud person. Proud of my name, my family . . . all of my family, that is, except my brother."

"Ah, yes. Dear old Edgar. Tell me, did you get him out of jail yet?"

"Yes. He's free."

"You don't look particularly happy about it."

"Frankly, I have little regard for my brother. He's done more to ruin the Burrell name than I would have thought any one person can do. He shames me, he shames my family, and if he vanished from this world, it would cause me no great sorrow."

"Well, you're forthright. I'll say that for you. And I agree. I believe that Edgar murdered my father. I want to see him punished for it."

"I know you do. And I can hardly blame you for your feelings. I must admit that Edgar probably had the motive, the opportunity, and the character—or lack thereof—to do such a dreadful thing."

"Look, just tell me why you're here today."

"I'm here for myself, for my father, for my mother. For all the Burrell family members who don't really deserve to have their names ruined by the actions of my brother."

"The actions of your brother, you say. Is that your way of confirming to me that Edgar killed my father?"

"I can't prove anything one way or another. Suffice it to say I can understand and sympathize with your suspicions about my brother. Which leads me to why I've come."

David clamped his mouth shut and stopped speaking. John wondered, perturbed, why people always waited to be prompted at moments such as this. "Go on, then."

"I've come to see if I might not be able to persuade you to let things go, so to speak . . . to perhaps accept the fact that nothing you or I or anyone else can do can bring your father back, and that to go on with the kind of inquiries and accusations you have will really only hurt a family that doesn't deserve it."

"Your own, you mean."

"Yes. But listen to me, John! Don't look at me like you are! You have to understand. My father is deeply hurt by all that's happened. Edgar has shamed him deeply. But worse than that, there's what's happened to my mother because of this. My dear mother, always a good, fine woman, but never strong . . . and now all the shame and whispers have ruined her. She's turned to drink. She never shows herself in public." All at once, all the haughty veneer was stripped away from David Burrell; he was plaintive and human, speaking from his heart. "I love my mother, John. She matters more to me than anyone else. I can't bear to see her hurt."

John, shocked to witness this baring of

David Burrell's rarely seen soul, felt an unexpected burst of sympathy. Also confusion. What was David asking of him?

"David, my purpose isn't to hurt anyone except whoever murdered my father. But you'll have to explain yourself a little more. What do you want from me?"

David Burrell's tongue snaked out and wet his lips. He cleared his throat, eyelids batting nervously. Reaching under his coat, he brought out a well-stuffed leather pouch. "Here," he said, handing it toward John. "Take it. There's money in there. Probably more than you've ever seen at one place. And it's all yours, if you'll only leave Larimont, quit asking all these questions . . . and let my family regain the peace that it's lost."

John stared silently. The silence became long enough to grow tense, but John showed no eagerness to break it.

"Well?" David Burrell asked. "Will you take it?"

"I should throw you out of here. And I ought to take your head off before I do."

David sputtered disbelievingly. "You're *refusing* me?"

"You think I'd let my father's murderer go unavenged just for a pouch of money?"

"What? I don't understand. . . . I mean, look how much I'm offering you!"

"You really *don't* understand, do you? For you it's all about your family, your worries, your reputation. The great Burrell name! And the rest of us, well, we're just there to be bought off. Hustled out of the way with a few well-placed dollars. Do you think my own father means less to me than your mother means to you, David? Do you really believe that?"

David gaped. "You *are* refusing me!"

"Indeed I am."

David Burrell visibly withdrew, drawing into himself, his face masking over with coldness, his eyes narrowing. "You'll regret this, John. You should have accepted my offer."

"Get out of here."

"I'll tell you what. I'll give you one more chance. If you'll accept my offer, then I'll—"

"Out!"

David Burrell stood, threw his head back, nostrils flaring like a horse's, and stomped out the door. John slammed it shut behind him.

Two days later, Sharon Bradley went to Victoria Rivers, as the recuperating woman lay back on her big four-poster bed, and spoke to her confidentially about John Kenton.

"He's changed, Victoria," she said. "Since Edgar Burrell got out of jail, John has shadowed him. And not secretly. Openly. He mocks

Edgar, challenges him, insults him. Calls him a murderer and openly declares that Edgar killed his father."

"I've already heard this," Victoria said. "Three people have called on me, telling me the same thing, and worrying about John."

"I'm worried, too."

"No more than I am. John's lost his perspective. He believes that he's proven that Edgar killed his father, but he's proven nothing of the sort. What he has is intuition and a reasonable likelihood of being right. But we still don't even know that Edgar really did it."

"I'm afraid John's going to antagonize Edgar until Edgar gets angry enough to kill him."

"Or to try. Maybe that's John's thinking. He wants Edgar to try to kill him, and give him the excuse to defend himself. Tell me, is John carrying his pistol all the time?"

"Constantly. And he all but defies the law to try to take it from him."

"Edgar will kill him. If this keeps up, it'll happen."

"Victoria, don't say that!"

"You fear the same yourself. You wouldn't be here if you didn't."

"But isn't there something we can do?"

"I don't think a thing we can say will persuade John to do anything differently than he is right now," Victoria said. "He's determined to avenge his father's death."

"Maybe Edgar will just get tired of it and go away."

"I don't know, Sharon. I wish he would. But Edgar Burrell doesn't seem the kind to run."

The next day, though, Edgar Burrell did run. The word spread through Larimont that he was gone, and Federick Burrell, though unwilling to answer questions, substantially confirmed the same in his silence.

When the news reached John Kenton, he was livid. He strode to the Larimont Bank even before it had opened its doors, and pounded on the door until Frederick Burrell, the only man inside, could no longer ignore it. He rose, left his office, and came to the door, staring at John through the glass.

"Open this door!" John shouted.

"The bank doesn't open for another half an hour," Burrell replied coolly.

"Open the door, damn you, or I'll kick it in!" John yelled back.

Burrell cocked one brow, sighed loudly, and twisted the latch. Then he stepped aside, wisely, for John shoved the door open so hard that Burrell would have been knocked down had he not gotten out of the way.

John had his pistol out and jammed against

Burrell's chin even before he'd gotten fully inside. The banker kept his calm, that same haughty brow arched as he gazed at his antagonist.

"Well, John, are you going to murder me in cold blood, right in the doorway of my bank?" he asked.

"I should, by all rights. I consider you almost as guilty as your son of my father's murder. You're the one who squelched the investigation! You're the one who looked out only for yourself and your family, and let Scruff Smithers take the blame for a crime he didn't do!"

"I believe you know a lot less about what happened than you pretend," Burrell said. "You've convinced yourself that you have all the answers, when in fact all you have are suppositions."

"The hell with this talk!" John bellowed. "Tell me where Edgar's gone!"

"I don't know. Edgar quit telling me his comings and goings many years ago."

"You're lying!"

"You think Edgar and I are close? You believe he'd come to me if he wanted to flee and not be tracked?"

"So that's what he's doing? Fleeing?"

"It would appear so to me. Please, John, can't you lower that pistol? I'm not going to do anything to endanger myself."

John chuckled bitterly. "No. I suppose you wouldn't." He lowered and holstered the pistol. "Self-protection. That's your forte. Now tell me where Edgar's gone."

"I told you already. I don't know."

"Then tell me where you think he might be."

"That's not anything I can guess."

"Has he run before, in the past?"

"A time or two he's had cause to make himself scarce."

"Where did he go then?"

"Really, I have no idea."

The pistol came out again and jammed hard against Burrell's Adam's apple. John shoved, sending the banker staggering backward. Meanwhile, John lifted up on the barrel, making the sight dig into the soft flesh beneath Burrell's chin. Burrell, gagging and sputtering, had to tilt his head back and go up on tiptoes as he backstepped.

"Talk to me, banker! Tell me where Edgar Burrell goes when he's on the run!"

Burrell's voice sounded high and squeaking. "He . . . he goes to the mountains . . . he makes camp, stays there alone until the trouble blows over . . . "

"The mountains? Outside of Larimont?"

"Yes."

"That's a lot of mountain country out there. Where exactly does he go?"

"I don't know."

John clicked back the hammer of his pistol.

"To the bluffs! The bluffs! That's usually where!"

John smiled and nodded. He thumbed down the hammer again and slowly withdrew the pistol. Burrell grabbed at his neck and sank to his knees, panting and sweating.

"I'll see you dead for that!" he snarled at John.

"Maybe you will. But you'll see your boy Edgar dead first," John replied. "After that, you do what you want—or try. All I care about is evening the score with the man who murdered my father."

John turned and walked out of the bank, still holding the pistol. Drew Roberts was crossing the street outside, toward him.

"John Kenton! Surrender that weapon!"

John lifted it, aimed it at the marshal's head, and clicked the hammer.

"I suggest you run like the bought-and-paid-for coward you are," he said to Roberts.

The marshal stared at him hatefully, but only a moment. Seeing the better part of discretion, he turned and walked back the way he'd come, while onlookers all around chuckled at the sight. The marshal had lost the respect of his town as soon as it had become evident that he was in Frederick Burrell's pocket. What had just transpired had sealed that disrespect into permanance. John knew it and was satisfied. Drew Roberts, quite likely, would leave this town before the sun set again, and not return.

John cast his eyes to the mountains. And by then, too, he hoped, Edgar Burrell would be dead.

Chapter Eighteen

The Larimont Bluffs.

It had been years since John Kenton had visited those sheer, imposing cliffs, which stood in a semicircular pattern around a deep crevasse in the mountains northwest of town. When had his last visit there been? He thought hard, and remembered, and the memory brought him a sad smile.

He'd taken a young woman there, back maybe a year before he'd left Larimont. Ephelia Green . . . a simple but appealing young woman who had been the object of a deep crush on John's part at the time. Without the knowledge of her parents or John's father, he'd gone with her to the bluffs on a Saturday and spent far too long there, getting back home after dark and finding major trouble awaiting him and her at their respective homes. He'd never been scolded so thoroughly by Bill Kenton as he had that day. But it had been worth it. Not a thing that was out of line had happened with Ephelia that day in the mountains. It had simply been an innocent, fun outing for the pair of them, and the last time he'd spent any time with her. Though his crush had lingered, hers hadn't. Five months later she'd married Jimmy Frost, and a few months past that, John Kenton had packed his bags and left Larimont.

He rode now toward the Larimont Bluffs, the trail so familiar, hardly changed by the passing of years. He thought back to visits to the bluffs years before that outing with Ephelia. As a boy he'd loved to make this trip, and Bill Kenton had taken him often. Sometimes they'd packed rifles and made a hunting trip of it. Other times they'd gone merely to hike and climb and enjoy the splendor of the mountains.

John glanced down at the Winchester booted in his saddle. A new rifle, hastily bought before he left town.

Today's journey to the bluffs was no mere hike, he thought grimly. This one was a hunting trip.

Secretly he was surprised at himself. This was out of character for him. He'd never been vengeful, never been prone to violence, never favored scoffing at the due process of law. Had some friend taken off on a similar course, he'd have tried to dissuade him. Told him to get a grip on his senses and not act like a fool.

Now the fool was John Kenton. And he didn't care. All he wanted was the satisfaction of vengeance. To take the life of the man who had taken the life of his father.

John rode on, well out of town, into the foothills and at last to the base of the looming mountains. The mountains had always seemed close enough to touch in Larimont; only when one actually journeyed to them did the several miles of distance between the town and the mountains reveal themselves.

By the time John's horse began plodding up the old, slanting trail toward the Larimont Bluffs, he was already weary, and the heat had gone off his anger. He paused a moment to let Kate rest, and to ask himself if he really wanted to continue. Might it be better to return to Larimont, make contact with a federal marshal or some state officer, and seek justice that way? That would be the more traditional route. The safe way.

Also the wrong way. For all John knew, Edgar Burrell was planning to leave the state completely. He might not even be at the Larimont Bluffs at all. Every moment's delay might be giving him the chance to put extra miles behind him. No, John didn't have time to take the traditional, unsure route to justice—unsure because such a man as Frederick Burrell surely held the power to influence politicians and courts in secret ways. There was only one thing to do, and that was to bring in Edgar Burrell himself.

No, he corrected himself. Not bring in. Bring *down*.

He realized that fate might be doing him a favor, if Edgar really was at the Larimont Bluffs. There, no witnesses were likely. There, John could do what justice demanded without fearing the consequences.

The thought, contrary to his usual character and way of thinking, strengthened and energized him. He urged Kate ahead, wanting to get every mile out of her that he could before having to dismount and take the hardest part of the trail ahead on foot.

He dreaded the exertion of that climb, recalling how difficult it had been even in the days of light and limber boyhood. No boy of Larimont had ever been able to make the climb up to Larimont Bluffs without growing winded. Except for one.

Edgar Burrell.

Kate had been left far behind, hobbled in a grassy area and no doubt glad to be through with her part of this ascension.

John struggled on, leaning into the slope, panting and sweating and hurting from exertion. He'd not realized how much stamina the relatively easy world of newspaper work had stolen from him. Several times he had to stop fully and catch his breath, taking advantage of those moments to scan the landscape in hope of seeing a smoke plume, or a flash of movement or color against the mountainous backdrop, or hearing some sound, to reveal the camp of Edgar Burrell.

The farther he went, the more unsure of himself John grew. What if Edgar wasn't here at all? Maybe Frederick Burrell had bluffed for his son. Maybe Edgar was hidden away in Burrell's own house. Maybe father and son were having a good laugh together over fool John Kenton, hauling his weary self up a steep mountain in search of someone not even there.

John looked up. He'd reached that certain spot along this way, the place where the Larimont Bluffs suddenly presented themselves in all their daunting splendor—high, striated faces of stone, two hundred feet high at places and sheer all the way down. A place of legends and folk tales, where Indians once fought one another, and where an early settler of the region reportedly threw himself to his death after accidentally shooting his own son during a hunt. John suddenly remembered something he'd forgotten . . . a gang of boys, including himself, gathering around a dark spot on a stone to stare at it, while none other than Edgar Burrell swore to them all that the dark place was what remained of the bloodstains left by that legendary, suicidal early settler.

John caught himself grinning at the memory, and made himself stop. He couldn't begin to think sentimentally, especially about anything involving Edgar Burrell. To do what needed doing, he had to keep his hatred pure and hot.

He put another foot forward and heaved himself farther up the trail, when a shot sounded and a slug slapped through the treetops ahead and spanged against a boulder.

"You won't let it go, will you, Kenton?"

Edgar Burrell's voice echoed off the bluffs, making it hard to discern exactly where it came from. John, who had ducked instinctively when the slug passed over, looked wildly around but could see nothing of Edgar.

"Why don't you leave me be? I didn't kill your father! Go away and let a man have some peace!"

"I'll trail you until I bring you down, Edgar!" John yelled back.

Edgar's answer was a shot, even higher-aimed than the first one.

"What's wrong, Edgar? Are you going blind in your old age? You're not even coming close!"

Another shot, just as wild. But John ducked all the same, and wondered what in the devil he was doing, taunting a man who was shooting at him. Maybe he was as crazy as Edgar himself.

"Go away, John!" Edgar yelled. "Leave me be! I want no trouble with you!"

John pondered this. Edgar was shooting at him, at the same time declaring he wanted no trouble.

But was he really shooting *at* him? Edgar was known as a good shot, even in boyhood. But these shots were flying very high, not really even coming close. And there was the fact that Edgar had fled Larimont rather than tried to track John down.

Maybe he really didn't want trouble.

John peered about, looking for Edgar. *Whether he wants trouble or not, he's found it. I'll not let my father's murderer go unpunished.*

"You going to go away, John? Or am I going to have to kill you?"

"You got that wrong," John yelled back. "It's me who'll kill you."

Another shot, as high as before . . . but this time John saw the powder flash, and picked out Edgar's hunched-over form among the rocks on a rugged slope across the crevasse from him.

John rose and scrambled to a safer place, a plan forming in his mind. Edgar saw him and fired again, but once more the shot was very high.

You ought to do better, Edgar, John thought. *You ought to shoot me while you can . . . because when I get closer to you, your life is over.*

"John?" Edgar called.

John grinned. Edgar had lost sight of him. That was good. It would give him more time to find a place he could aim from, find the best shot . . .

Something in him faltered. Could he do this, really? Could he line his sights up on a man and squeeze the trigger?

He had to. This was the killer of Bill Kenton. This was a man who would probably escape justice forever unless justice found him right here and now.

"John? You hiding from me?"

John didn't answer. He kept climbing, his eye on a notched rock slightly to the right and above him. A good niche for a sniper.

The air was thin, and John's heart was already hammering from the exertion of the climb and the terror of being shot at, however indirectly. Still he kept climbing.

He was careful as he crept toward the notched rock. At one point he'd inevitably be exposed to Edgar's view, assuming Edgar happened to look in the right direction at the right time.

John didn't want Edgar to see where he wound

up. The key to a successful shot would be surprise. If he could make it to that rock unseen, he could end this business quite summarily.

John climbed on, carefully and far more slowly than he wished he could. Edgar called for him, scanned the landscape, and fired the occasional skyward shot.

The Larimont Bluffs loomed above, their shadows moving and darkening as the day began to wane.

John realized he had to move faster. Darkness would fall fast here and rob him of his chance. He increased his speed, praying that Edgar would not see him.

He stayed in hiding as long as he could, then reached a place where he had no option but to cross over an open face of stone toward the notched rock that was his goal. He paused there, took three deep breaths, got a grip on his rifle, and began his scramble.

John was halfway across the stone face when Edgar's rifle spoke loudly. He felt a sharp sting in his right calf. His foot went out from under him, his balance vanished, and he tumbled to the right, down the slope, rolling and tumbling.

He lost his rifle somewhere along the way, hearing it clatter off down the stone slope. His head pounded hard against a boulder, and his body dislodged a mass of gravel that poured and danced down the slope all around him.

He thought, in the midst of it all, that he heard another shot, but he couldn't be sure.

He tried to find a handhold and stop his tumble, but succeeded only in abrading his hands, scraping off hide to the point of drawing blood. Then his body pitched into open space, and he turned in the air, seeing the world open up below him, a seemingly vast chasm with no bottom.

He screamed as his body turned again, and fell.

Chapter Nineteen

His right leg, if not broken, was severely sprained, but John was hardly sensible enough to recognize the fact. All he knew was that he was lying flat on something hard, and in a most uncomfortable position. And he knew he'd fallen. Just how far, he wasn't sure.

He'd struck hard, and though he couldn't be sure of it, he believed he'd been knocked unconscious a few moments after the impact. Even now he wasn't fully aware, feeling stunned. It was difficult to think . . . but something nagged at him, telling him that he was in danger if he lay here much longer.

Danger . . .

He looked around, turning his head slowly because his neck, like most of the rest of him, hurt.

Something . . . a noise. Something drawing near . . .

With a wince he managed to turn his head, then to roll over. He let out a long, low moan, his leg throbbing with sharp pain as he turned. His new position, though, gave him a view up the long slope he'd tumbled down. He'd hit a lip of rock at the bottom that had pitched him out into open space, and he'd thought he was going to fall a long distance. Instead he'd landed on a wide ledge he'd not been able to see from above. It had saved his life, but not without leaving him quite battered.

Someone was coming down the slope, scooting and scuffing and sliding, with a rifle gripped in one hand.

Now he remembered what the danger was . . . who it was. Edgar Burrell.

Edgar, coming down the slope toward him.

John knew he couldn't remain where he was. If Edgar reached him, as he would in moments, he'd be a dead man.

Had to rise, had to find his own rifle. Had to defend himself . . .

John steeled himself, preparing for the pain he knew he'd feel. With a groan and superhuman effort, he pushed upright, pulling his left leg up and under him, and rising by its power rather than that of his throbbing right leg.

He was dizzy, dazed, and it was hard to remain upright. He staggered, and in so doing, put weight onto his right leg without meaning to do so.

He yelled and fell to the right, toward the sharp rim of the ledge.

"Hold still, Kenton!" Edgar yelled at him from halfway up the slope. "Hold still. . . . I ain't going to hurt you!"

Of course you won't, John thought. *You took how many shots at me, threatened me . . . and now you don't plan to hurt me?*

He tried to rise again, but it was harder this time. He accidentally rolled a little farther toward the ledge rim.

Edgar Burrell was much closer now, coming down faster, almost falling himself now.

John sensed the open space beside him and knew he must move away from it. He couldn't fall, not now, not after having come so close to that fate already.

He wondered where his rifle was. Maybe it hadn't been as lucky as he and had pitched over the edge of the chasm already.

Edgar was closer now, shouting at him to lie still.

John would not lie still. He wouldn't die this way, just lying there, waiting for his fate.

With another groan and effort he pushed up. . . .

The rim of the ledge, nothing but weak, fractured rock, gave way beneath him. He fell, groping. . . .

Somehow he caught himself. But the pain was unbearable. He was hanging now by his hands, holding to the unstable, thin edge of the broken ledge, his legs swinging out in space beneath him. His injured right leg throbbed even more painfully than before; his body felt as if it weighed half a ton and would at any moment tear his gripping fingers out by their roots.

He knew he shouldn't look down, but he did, and saw the ground two hundred feet below him. A sheer, straight fall, with jagged rocks below.

He looked up again, fighting a fast-coming sense of faintness. No, God. No. Not like this.

He looked up again. Edgar Burrell was coming down at a near scramble, barely keeping hold of his rifle. But he did keep hold, and in moments was directly above John, standing on the ledge, looking down at him as he swung over space. The rifle was still in his hands.

"So what will it be?" John asked, voice

straining. "Will you shoot me, or just let me fall?"

"Neither," Edgar said, kneeling and laying his rifle aside. "I'm going to pull you up, John. Hang on."

John was so surprised, he almost let go. "What?"

"I'm going to pull you up! Are you hard of hearing?" Edgar lay on his belly, bracing himself by anchoring his feet between boulders. Reaching over, he grabbed John's wrists, wrapping his hands around tightly, just as John's fingers were about to let go of their own accord.

"You're going to drop me," John said, staring up at Edgar's face. "You're going to tell me to let go, then you're going to drop me."

"If I wanted you dead, I could have shot you before. Or I could have just left you hanging here so you'd fall when your strength ran out. I don't want to kill you, John."

"I don't trust you. . . . "

"Do you have any choice?"

John knew he didn't. If he was to live, it would be through Edgar's efforts. If Edgar intended to let him fall, there was nothing John could do to stop him. And without Edgar's help, he'd fall anyway.

He had nothing to lose in trusting Edgar, and maybe his life to gain.

John let go of the ledge.

Immediately Edgar's face twisted into a grimace of effort as John's full weight transferred itself to his grip. John stared into that twisted face, wondering if at any moment it might break into a dark grin, then recede swiftly from him as he was allowed to drop. It didn't happen. Edgar, through gritted teeth, urged him to hang on, to find a foothold if he could, and to help him as he tried to pull John up.

It came to John quite clearly, as he hung there, that Edgar really was trying to save him. The same man who had threatened him and fired his rifle—the same man John himself had been eager to kill—was now trying to keep him alive. It made little sense.

John groped with his feet, seeking a toehold. Edgar's hands were beginning to tremble, his grip on John's wrists slipping slightly. John knew Edgar could never get him back on the ledge alone. He'd have to have help.

But the more John moved his feet—in actual fact, his left foot, for his injured right leg hurt far too badly for him to use—the harder it was for Edgar to continue to hold him. Meanwhile, a new fear arose. If the ledge had broken once, might it do so again, especially now that the weight of two men was upon it?

John's foot touched a rock, found a small crack. It slipped away from him, but he guided his foot back and managed to wedge the toe of his boot in the crack. Pushing up, he saw Edgar grin slightly, and they actually made progress, John edging up a little, and strengthening his hold on Edgar, and Edgar's on him, at the same time.

"We'll make it, John," Edgar said. "Just keep pushing."

Together they worked, John giving it all he had, Edgar doing the same. By inches, John moved up. Edgar, meanwhile, edged back, using his braced feet for leverage.

"Soon," he said. "Soon you'll be able to take hold and pull yourself over."

There was a cracking sound, a slight shifting of the rock of the ledge.

"It's breaking," John said, finding his voice a whisper. "The ledge is breaking."

"No," Edgar said. "No, John. It's just a crack in the stone, that's all. It's plenty strong enough to hold us. Come on, now. Pull!"

Then, with a mutual effort so great it drew a yell from the throats of both men, they made a great pull and heave, and the next thing John knew, he was holding to the rim of the ledge again, and Edgar was reaching over, gripping his clothing, pulling up. . . .

John rolled over onto the ledge, lay there a moment, gasping for breath, actually fainting for a second or two. Then Edgar stirred him to rise, pulled him back to a thicker, safer portion of the ledge.

John lay on his back, blinking, looking at the sky, now beginning to darken.

"Why?" he asked. "First you shoot at me, then you save me."

"I didn't shoot at you," Edgar replied. "I shot above your head. I was trying to scare you away."

"I came here to kill you, you know. Even when I fell down the slope, I was trying to get to a place where I could shoot you."

"I figured. That's why I put that particular bullet a little closer to you."

"I thought you'd shot me. I felt a sting in my leg."

"I didn't hit you. Maybe it was some chipped stone from where the bullet struck."

John sat up and looked at Edgar, who was crouched, sweating and breathless, about four feet away, looking back at him.

"Edgar, my father—"

"I really didn't kill him, John. I'm not lying to you." He paused. "Do you believe me?"

John thought about it. "I didn't. Now, I think, I do."

"I hope you do. Because it's the truth. I've done many a wrong thing in my time. I robbed my own father's bank. I sent the very woman I love into a life little better than that of a common whore, and that with my own father. Me and the Horner brothers tried to scare you and Victoria and poor old Scruff's niece into letting it all alone. I tried to bribe you. But it was all to cover up the bank robbery and about June. That's all. I never killed your father."

"Why did you run out here to the bluffs?"

"I wasn't trying to run. I came here for the same reason I always have, all my life. To escape for just a little while, and to think. To try to figure out what I need to do." He paused. "And what's really going on. And after I got here, I realized I've got a lot to make up for. I've done some foolish and wrong things . . . and in a way, all this is my fault. None of it would have happened if me and the Horners hadn't decided to rob Pap's bank." He chuckled. "It seemed quite a joke at the time. Rob Pap's bank, and leave him in a situation where he can't do anything about it without having the whole world learn that he's been dallying with a gal young enough to be his daughter." In the gathering gloom, Edgar paused and looked down. "Poor June. She'd do anything I asked of her . . . and I asked all the wrong things. God forgive me."

"Why the change of attitude, Edgar?"

"Because of June. When she died, that changed everything. It took me some time to see it, but everything was different. It was the end."

"Edgar, if you didn't kill my father, if it wasn't you who shot through the window and killed June . . . then who did?"

"I didn't know. . . . I think I do now."

"Tell me."

"I think it's somebody who cares a hell of a lot about the good name of the Burrell family."

John paused. "David."

"Yes. And if I know David, he's probably still worried about our precious family reputation. And if he's gone this far to try to protect it . . . "

"Edgar . . . David is still in Larimont. And so are Victoria, and Sharon."

"That's why we need to get back there, and go pay a call on them. Before David decides to do the same."

"I can't walk, Edgar. My leg . . . "

"Reckon we'll have to splint it."

"But even then, how can I make it all the way back down?"

"I'll help you. Down's always easier than up."

"Edgar . . . I'm sorry I doubted you. I really thought you were the one."

"I'd have thought the same in your shoes. Now hush up, and help me find something to brace that leg with. It'll be dark soon, and nigh on to midnight before we can make it back to Larimont."

Chapter Twenty

Victoria Rivers stirred in her bed, vaguely conscious of the clock in the hallway having just chimed midnight. And something else, too . . . something she couldn't quite grasp.

She rolled to one side and resettled her head in her pillow. The clock ticked repetitively, hypnotic and faint, and she began to sink farther into sleep. But a moment later she heard, or maybe just sensed, something odd . . . and opened her eyes.

She sat up.

"Sharon?" she said softly.

There was no reply, but it seemed to her that something in the shadows beyond the open door of her room shifted and changed. There was a whisper of noise, almost below the level of hearing.

"Sharon, is that you?"

No answer.

"Sharon, are you sleepwalking?"

No answer again . . . but this time she was certain something moved out there.

Victoria's heart began to hammer. She stared out the doorway, looking hard and listening, and trying not to breathe very loudly.

For a full minute she remained as she was, not moving, hardly blinking. Then slowly she turned her head to the left and looked toward her wardrobe in the corner. Beside it, unseen in the night shadows, leaned her shotgun. Loaded. Hardly ever touched, but always kept at that place, just in case she needed it.

She wondered if she needed it now.

Victoria snapped her head back around, having heard something beyond the doorway.

Reflexively, she held her breath.

But still she heard the sound of breathing.

It was all she needed to hear. Rising quickly, she ran toward the wardrobe and grabbed the shotgun, as through the doorway came a dark, phantom figure, racing toward her.

Her hand closed on the cold stock of the shotgun. She yanked it up, tried to turn, but a hand closed like an overtightened vise on her right shoulder and pushed her, making her stumble against the wall.

The man, whoever it was, shoved against her, slamming her against the wall panel, crushing her, muttering curses vaguely in a whispered voice that sounded familiar. She smelled his breath and the alcoholic stench it bore.

She was trapped, her hand still on the shotgun, but with no room available to let her hoist it.

She felt the man's hand grope down her arm, find her hand and the shotgun stock it gripped. He cursed again—and she knew who it was then—and took hold of the shotgun, pulling it away from her violently. He let go of her at the same moment and backed away.

"Please," Victoria said. "Please, David, don't kill me!"

David Burrell laughed. "Kill you. Why would I want to kill you, Victoria?" The shotgun was raised, aiming at her. She could barely make it out in the darkness. "Why would I want to kill someone just because they're determined to destroy my family and its reputation? What motive would that give me, hmm?"

His sarcasm deepened her fear. This young man was in a mental state that was quite dangerous. Victoria knew then, with certainty, that this was who had killed Bill Kenton. She knew why, too. Bill Kenton had dared to probe into a crime that had Burrell family fingerprints on it. And he hadn't backed away. He'd been ready to expose a bank robbery performed by Edgar Burrell, and in so doing, bring shame on the Burrell family's precious name.

Victoria wanted to cringe, to beg, to pray aloud. . . . She wanted to scream for Sharon, upstairs, to come down and save her. But what could Sharon do against a man armed with a shotgun, and maybe other weapons besides?

She forced herself to maintain control. . . . she had to think, to get out of this in whatever way she could. Cringing and begging wouldn't work.

"You should have left it alone," David said. "You should have never had anything to do with John Kenton. He's a fool. As big a fool as his father was. That's why I had to get rid of him, you know. Bill Kenton didn't have the common sense, the common *decency*, to leave a good family's reputation alone. He had to be gotten rid of, before he ruined everything."

Hard as it was to do, Victoria said what she knew she must. "Yes . . . yes, you're right, of course."

"You *agree* with me?"

"I . . . understand you. I can see why you felt as you did."

David Burrell's face was invisible to her, but

she could sense the confusion it surely would have revealed had she been able to see it.

"You're trying to toy with me," he said. "You know I've come to kill you—you know I *have* to kill you—and you're trying to stop me."

He was certainly right about that. "David, you don't need to kill me. I can help you."

"Help me? How?"

"I can persuade John Kenton to stop asking questions. I can convince him that someone else killed his father. I can make him go away and stop bothering your family."

A pause. "You'd do that?"

"Yes, David. Of course I would. I like you, David. I always have. I didn't realize we were causing you so much pain."

His voice sounded weak, rather pitiful. "There has been pain. So much. But not all your fault, or even John Kenton's. That I have to admit."

She sensed something in him growing calmer, less dangerous. Thank God. She'd try to keep him talking . . . for when he was talking, he was unlikely to be shooting. "What do you mean?"

"My father, and Edgar . . . both of them should be ashamed of themselves. The things they've done! The risks they've taken with the family's good name." He paused. "My father was doing a very wrong thing, you know. With June Layne . . . the harlot!"

"Oh. I see."

"Yes. It was shameful. I don't think he knew that I knew. But I did. And I was so ashamed. . . . I despised what he was doing. If word had gotten out, can you imagine what that would have done to our family's reputation? Can you *imagine*?"

He was beginning to sound worked up again. *Please, David*, she thought, *stay calm. Please.*

"I had to kill Bill Kenton. But my father never knew. I never told him."

Victoria felt she should speak, but knew nothing to say.

"Father has thought all along that Edgar killed Bill Kenton. Did you know that? It's true. He assumed that Edgar did it, and so Father forced Alexander Layne to tell the story against Scruff Smithers, to keep himself safe, and to keep his love affair with June Layne a secret. That was Father's motivation, you see—looking out for himself. He doesn't really care much about Edgar, but he did believe that if Edgar was arrested for the murder, he'd reveal the truth about June Layne and Father. And he couldn't have that. No, indeed."

David had lowered the shotgun a little, but not fully. Victoria was feeling weak, faint, but dared not move from where she was.

"You know," David mused, "this whole sorry business has about exhausted me. I've been so busy, lurking around in the background, watching, doing what had to be done to protect my family. When John Kenton showed up, asking his questions, poking his nose into my family's business, I began to follow him. Everywhere he went, whatever he did, I was there, watching. It was hard, sometimes, to do it without being detected. But I succeeded. There was hardly a move he made, hardly a place he went, that I wasn't watching, and following . . . and doing whatever needed doing to try to stop the terrible damage he was doing. I watched him almost constantly.

"And I watched the people he talked to. Like Lawrence Poteet. I saw the way Lawrence was beginning to act, his suspicious manner, those shifting, worrying eyes of his. . . . I knew he was becoming a threat. And when he took John into his home, talked to him, I knew he had to be removed. So I removed him. Hated to do it, really. I've always been fond of Lawrence." He paused; she sensed him looking at her. "I've always been fond of you, too."

Under the circumstances, she found little comfort in that.

"David," she suggested, "would you like to move elsewhere, someplace we can be more comfortable while we talk?"

"I'm fine where I am."

"But I'm not. . . . I was injured recently, you know. I've been mostly bedfast ever since, and it's hard to stand here."

To her surprise, David Burrell laughed. "You looked plenty strong enough when you sprang out of that bed and ran for the shotgun."

"I was scared, David. You frightened me. I'm still scared."

"I'm sorry it has to be this way."

"It doesn't. I think I can help you, David. You don't need to hurt me. You don't need to hurt anyone else at all."

"Help me? How?"

"Come into the kitchen with me. I'll make us coffee. There's some bread in there, I think. Sharon baked two loaves this afternoon. We can eat and talk."

"How can you help me, though?"

"I can cause all the questions to stop. I can make John stop everything he's doing. I can make all this go away."

He paused. "No. No. It's too late. People are already dead because of this . . . people I've killed. Bill Kenton. Lawrence Poteet. And June. Poor June. I didn't realize it was her. As much as I despise her for the harlot she was, I didn't mean to kill her."

"Who were you trying to kill, then? Me? Sharon Bradley?"

"Either of you would have done nicely. And don't think ill of me for saying such a thing. It's not really my choice, you know. I've been forced to all this."

"Let's go to the kitchen, Edgar."

"No. We need to end this right now."

"Are you going to shoot me right in my own house?"

"No." He cracked the shotgun and removed its shells. Pocketing them, he tossed the weapon onto Victoria's bed. Reaching beneath his jacket, he pulled out something that Victoria couldn't really see, though a sliver of moonlight caught it and she detected the fast gleam of shining metal.

"I have to be quieter than a shotgun would be," he said. "We can't awaken Sharon, you know."

He raised his hand, the unidentified weapon in it glittering again in the shaft of moonlight.

Victoria screamed, as loudly as she could, and ran straight at David Burrell with her arms extended. She hit him in the chest, knocking him down, then ran right across him.

He cursed and swung his weapon at her. It missed, but she heard a chopping noise as it struck the floor, like a blade sinking into wood.

Victoria ran, crying out for Sharon.

Just ahead was the front door of her house. She could exit the house, raise a cry outside and escape safely . . .

But she couldn't, not with Sharon upstairs, probably not fully realizing yet what was happening.

Victoria turned up the staircase, running and shouting. David Burrell came into the hallway below, cursing. His weapon was in his hand. Victoria glanced down as she reached the top of the stairs and saw, in the brighter moonlight in the front hall, that what he held was a meat cleaver.

She screamed again.

A meat cleaver. David Burrell had come here planning to hack her to death, then Sharon.

Sharon was already standing in the doorway of her room when Victoria rounded the corner toward her.

"Victoria, what is—"

"Go back inside!" Victoria yelled, hearing David coming up the stairs already. "Go inside and close the door!"

Victoria was almost on top of Sharon by the time she finished the sentence. Sharon backed inside quickly, Victoria bursting in past her, and slammed the door shut. Victoria turned and latched it, then twisted the key in the lock. Grabbing a chair, she shoved the back of it beneath the doorknob and jammed it in place.

"Victoria, what's happening?"

"David Burrell's out there. . . . It's he who killed Bill, and Lawrence Poteet, and June—"

Something slammed hard against the door. David Burrell, throwing himself against the panels so hard that the door bowed and seemed about to pop off its hinges.

Sharon screamed.

"Pile more furniture against the door!" Victoria demanded. "Hurry!"

Together she and Sharon pushed a heavy chest of drawers toward the door. They jammed it hard against the edge of the door.

On the other side, David Burrell was cursing and pounding. Victoria and Sharon scrambled for other items of furniture, trying to increase the weight of the barricade.

A loud chopping sound echoed from the door, followed by another, and another, and suddenly the wood splintered.

David Burrell was chopping at the door with the cleaver.

Sharon screamed again, cringing back, falling to her knees and covering her face with her hands.

Victoria went to her, grabbed her, shook her. "Stop it! We can stop him if we keep our heads and work together."

"How? How?"

Victoria looked wildly around the dark room. Her eye fell on a pair of kerosene lamps standing on the mantelpiece.

The hacking of the door continued, splinters ripping out with each blow.

Victoria ran to the mantel and grabbed one lamp. She pulled the globe free and tossed it aside; it shattered on the floor. Yanking out the wick mechanism, she grabbed a block of matches off the mantel.

Sharon grasped what Victoria was doing and went through the same routine with the other lamp, as the door continued to be hacked away.

She and Victoria moved together to the door. Though much of it was covered by the furniture they had put in place, a couple of inches of the base of the door was still accessible. Together they poured their kerosene onto the floor; it ran out beneath the door to pool around David Burrell's feet.

Victoria prayed that the young man, in his frenzy, would not notice the kerosene.

Breathing a prayer, Victoria broke off a match, struck it, and lit the kerosene.

Flame caught and traveled along the kerosene, passing under the door.

David Burrell howled like a wounded beast. The hacking on the door ceased. His screams continued out in the hall as he danced and slapped at the flames crawling up his legs.

Victoria looked at Sharon. Their plan had worked, but at best it would keep David Burrell back only a few moments. And now flames were crawling up the door. The same effort that had temporarily driven back David Burrell was also likely to trap them in this room.

The upper part of the door splintered seconds later. In one great burst, David Burrell had hammered the panel away. In the semi-darkness, illuminated only by infiltrating moonlight and the weird flicker of the kerosene flames, they saw him.

David Burrell ignored the flames now, clambering right through them, and through the shattered door, onto the top of the chest of drawers. He leaped from it onto the floor, the cleaver in his right hand. Cursing, he shoved aside the furniture that had blocked the door, strengthened by his fury.

A line of flame crawled up the left leg of his trousers. He noticed it, beat it out quickly, hardly seeming to care. He glared at the two women.

"You're dead. Both of you, you're dead. And when I find John Kenton, he's dead, too. None of you are even fit to live . . . spreading stories about my family, hurting our reputation, not caring how such things make my poor mother feel! I hate you! I hate all of you!"

He was upon them in a moment, shoving Sharon aside, making her fall. He tripped Victoria, came down hard upon her, pinning her with his weight. He brought up the cleaver and brought it down.

Victoria somehow managed to pull to one side and avoid the blow. The cleaver bit into the floor beside her. David Burrell cursed and pulled it free. He raised it again.

"David!"

David froze at the unexpected sound of the male voice. He turned, let go of Victoria, and came to his feet.

The flames had died away at the doorway, the wood having not fully caught. In that smoking doorway stood Edgar Burrell, rifle in hand. He stared back at his younger brother.

"No, David. No. Let her alone."

"Why the hell should I? Where did you come from?"

"From the Larimont Bluffs. Where I was try-ing to hide. . . . But I can't hide anymore. The things I've done have cost the lives of too many good people, the best of them being the very woman I loved. No more of that, David. Let's you and me leave this be right now, and stop before things get worse."

"But the family, Edgar . . . the *family*! Do you not care about the things these people are say-ing, the way it hurts Mother, the way it ruins our family name . . . No, no. I suppose you *don't* care. You've never cared! If not for the way you've behaved, none of this would have happened. None of it."

"I know," Edgar said. "I know. And that's why I came back. Because I'm going to face what I've done."

A voice called from downstairs. Sharon

glanced at Victoria. John's voice! Had he followed Edgar here?

"I'll kill you, too!" David said to his brother. "It's your fault as much as anyone's!"

He raised the cleaver and advanced toward Edgar.

Edgar backed up a step and raised the rifle. But he hesitated, didn't fire. David moved in, swinging.

Edgar screamed; the rifle fell to the floor, and with it, three of his fingers.

Clutching his blood-spurting hand, he backed off into the hall and flopped down onto his rump. David advanced and began hacking. Edgar tried to get away, but David was relentless.

When he'd hacked his brother seven or eight times, he tossed the cleaver back over his shoulder into the bedroom, reached to Edgar's neck, and began to choke him.

Up the stairs came John Kenton, all but crawling, dragging his splinted leg, unable to move fast enough to reach the Burrell brothers.

"No!" he yelled. "No, David! Don't kill him!"

David jerked his head up and glared at John, his eyes wild in the moonlight, fired with hate. . . .

And even as John watched, that fire died, instantly, as Sharon Bradley emerged from the bedroom with the cleaver in her hand, and brought it down with skull-splitting force onto and into the head of David Burrell.

He froze, the metal buried in his brain, gave one twitch, and fell to the side, dying with his eyes open.

Edgar Burrell, brutally cut, bleeding profusely, turned his head and stared into the open eyes of his dead brother. He drew in a deep, slow breath, let it out. He did not draw another.

Chapter Twenty-one

One week later

John leaned on the cane that had become his steady companion over the last several days, as his sprained and bruised leg slowly healed. He looked at the gravestone of his father and thought of all the years past, and the years he'd anticipated he'd still have the pleasure of his father's company.

Life was a strange, unpredictable thing. A man never knew how long he'd be privileged to call his blessings his own.

John looked up and smiled at Sharon Bradley, who stood at the gate of the graveyard, respectfully giving John time alone with his father's memory.

If a man didn't know how long his blessings would remain his own, maybe the lesson to be learned was to waste no time in taking full advantage of them.

He hobbled over to Sharon, who slipped her arm into his and helped bear his weight as they walked together.

"Frederick Burrell is leaving town, you know. Taking his wife with him. I heard it from Victoria this morning."

"Yes. She told me, too. You know, I feel sorry for them, in a way. None of this was anything they planned to happen. Just a series of bad circumstances—one son being basically worthless and amoral, robbing his own father's bank, misusing his lover, the other son being, ultimately, a drunkard and near madman, obsessed with family pride and protecting his beloved mother's delicate feelings. But who would have dreamed he would go as far as he did?"

"I'm glad it's over."

"So am I."

"Where will you go now, John?"

"I don't know. I have a job to return to . . . if I decide to."

"Might you decide differently?"

"I could be persuaded."

"What are you thinking, John?"

"I'm thinking that maybe, just maybe, a small newspaper might be able to survive in Larimont. Not that I'd have much money to hire a staff of workers. Probably just me . . . and maybe one other person."

"I can think of a possible applicant."

John smiled and patted her hand.

"Coming home to Larimont . . . I should have done it soon0er, while my father was still with me. So often we make the important decisions too late."

"And sometimes we don't," she replied.

They walked together, slowly, down the dusty road and toward the town. The breeze was rising with the sun. It was going to be, as best could be told, quite a fine day.

THE GALLOWSMAN

WILL CADE

Ben Woolard is a man ready to start over. The life he's leaving behind is filled with ghosts and pain. He lost his wife and children, and his career as a Union spy during the war still doesn't sit quite right with him, even if the man sent to the gallows by his testimony was a murderer. But now Ben's finally sobered up, moved west to Colorado, and put the past behind him. But sometimes the past just won't stay buried. And, as Ben learns when folks start telling him that the man he saw hanged is alive and in town—sometimes those ghosts come back.

___4452-8 $4.50 US/$5.50 CAN

Dorchester Publishing Co., Inc.
P.O. Box 6640
Wayne, PA 19087-8640

Please add $1.75 for shipping and handling for the first book and $.50 for each book thereafter. NY, NYC, and PA residents, please add appropriate sales tax. No cash, stamps, or C.O.D.s. All orders shipped within 6 weeks via postal service book rate. Canadian orders require $2.00 extra postage and must be paid in U.S. dollars through a U.S. banking facility.

Name_____
Address_____
City_____State_____Zip_____
I have enclosed $_____ in payment for the checked book(s).
Payment <u>must</u> accompany all orders. ❏ Please send a free catalog.

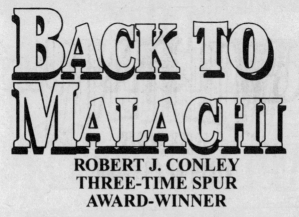

BACK TO MALACHI

ROBERT J. CONLEY
THREE-TIME SPUR
AWARD-WINNER

Charlie Black is a young half-breed caught between two worlds. He is drawn to the promise of the white man's wealth, but torn by his proud heritage as a Cherokee. Charlie's pretty young fiancée yearns for the respectability of a Christian marriage and baptized children. But Charlie can't forsake his two childhood friends, Mose and Henry Pathkiller, who live in the hills with an old full-blooded Indian named Malachi. When Mose runs afoul of the law, Charlie has to choose between the ways of his fiancée and those of his friends and forefathers. He has to choose between surrender and bloodshed.

___4277-0 $3.99 US/$4.99 CAN

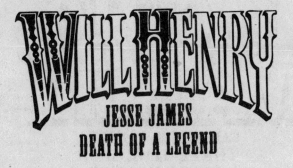

WILL HENRY

JESSE JAMES
DEATH OF A LEGEND

Beneath the bandanna, underneath the legend, Jesse James was a wild and wicked man: a sinister and brutal outlaw who blazed a trail of crime and violence through the lawless West. Ripping the mask off the mysterious Jesse James, Will Henry's *Death Of A Legend* is a novel as tough and savage as the man himself. Only a great Western writer like Henry could tell the real story of the infamous bandit Jesse James.

_3990-7 $4.99 US/$6.99 CAN

Dorchester Publishing Co., Inc.
P.O. Box 6640
Wayne, PA 19087-8640

Please add $1.75 for shipping and handling for the first book and $.50 for each book thereafter. NY, NYC, and PA residents, please add appropriate sales tax. No cash, stamps, or C.O.D.s. All orders shipped within 6 weeks via postal service book rate. Canadian orders require $2.00 extra postage and must be paid in U.S. dollars through a U.S. banking facility.

Name_____
Address_____
City_____ State_____ Zip_____
I have enclosed $_____ in payment for the checked book(s).
Payment <u>must</u> accompany all orders. ☐ Please send a free catalog.

Last Chance

DEE MARVINE

Mattie Hamil is on a frantic journey west. On her own, with only her grit and determination to see her through, she has to find her charming gambler of a fiancé, and she has to do it fast—before her pregnancy shows. From a steamboat along the Missouri River to the rough-and-tumble post-gold-rush town of Last Chance, Montana, Mattie's trek leads her through danger and sorrow, friendship and joy. But even after she finds her fiancé, no bend in the trail leads to what she expected.

___4475-7 $4.99 US/$5.99 CAN

THE MUSTANGERS

GARY McCARTHY

In Nevada in the early 1860s, an increasingly profitable trade is springing up. It is called mustanging—the breaking and selling of rogue horses to the highest bidder. When Pete Sills, an eager apprentice mustanger, signs on at the Cross T Ranch, all he wants is to learn the trade. But as soon as he meets Candy, the ranch owner's daughter, all that changes. Now he wants her. But to win her he first has to capture Sun Dancer, the fabulous palomino that Candy has her heart set on. And that means more trouble for Pete than he can ever imagine . . . and a lesson about pride and courage that he will never forget.

___4518-4 $3.99 US/$4.99 CAN

WILD ROSE of RUBY CANYON

JOHN D. NESBITT

At first homesteader Henry Sommers is pleased when his neighbor Van O'Leary starts dropping by. After all, friends come in handy out on the Wyoming plains. But it soon becomes clear that O'Leary has some sort of money-making scheme in the works and doesn't much care how the money is made. Henry wants no part of his neighbor's dirty business, but freeing himself of O'Leary is almost as difficult as climbing out of quicksand . . . and just as dangerous.

___4520-6 $3.99 US/$4.99 CAN

Dorchester Publishing Co., Inc.
P.O. Box 6640
Wayne, PA 19087-8640

Please add $1.75 for shipping and handling for the first book and $.50 for each book thereafter. NY, NYC, and PA residents, please add appropriate sales tax. No cash, stamps, or C.O.D.s. All orders shipped within 6 weeks via postal service book rate. Canadian orders require $2.00 extra postage and must be paid in U.S. dollars through a U.S. banking facility.

Name_____
Address_____
City_____State_____Zip_____
I have enclosed $_____ in payment for the checked book(s).
Payment <u>must</u> accompany all orders. ❑ Please send a free catalog.
CHECK OUT OUR WEBSITE! www.dorchesterpub.com

THE WHITE CHIP

CHIP

NELSON C. NYE

The Lost Dutchman is the most fabled gold mine of the Old West. Hundreds of hopefuls have risked everything to find it—many never coming back. When an unlikely caravan finds the cleverly sealed-off entrance, the dizzying wealth is theirs for the taking—if they can retrieve it from the middle of an active volcano.

___4473-0 $4.50 US/$5.50 CAN

Dorchester Publishing Co., Inc.
P.O. Box 6640
Wayne, PA 19087-8640

Please add $1.75 for shipping and handling for the first book and $.50 for each book thereafter. NY, NYC, and PA residents, please add appropriate sales tax. No cash, stamps, or C.O.D.s. All orders shipped within 6 weeks via postal service book rate. Canadian orders require $2.00 extra postage and must be paid in U.S. dollars through a U.S. banking facility.

Name_____

Address_____

City_____State_____Zip_____

I have enclosed $_____ in payment for the checked book(s).

Payment <u>must</u> accompany all orders. ❑ Please send a free catalog.

CHECK OUT OUR WEBSITE! www.dorchesterpub.com